PENGUIN BOOKS

MOMO

Michael Ende was born in Garmisch-Partenkirchen, Germany, in 1929. After attending drama school from 1948 to 1950, he worked variously as an actor, a writer of sketches and plays, a director of the Volkstheater in Munich, and a film critic for the Bavarian broadcasting company. His first novel for children, *Jim Knopf and Lukas the Engine Driver*, was published in Germany in 1960 to great popular and critical acclaim, and both radio and television series based on the *Jim Knopf* books were soon produced. He is also the author of *The Neverending Story*, which was first published in Germany in 1979, and immediately became the number one bestseller. *The Neverending Story* is also available in Penguin Books.

MOMO

By Michael Ende

Translated by J. Maxwell Brownjohn

PENGUIN BOOKS

PENGUIN BOOKS
Viking Penguin Inc., 40 West 23rd Street,
New York, New York 10010, U.S.A.
Penguin Books Ltd, Harmondsworth, Middlesex, England
Penguin Books Australia Ltd, Ringwood, Victoria, Australia
Penguin Books Canada Limited, 2801 John Street,
Markham, Ontario, Canada L3R 1B4
Penguin Books (N.Z.) Ltd, 182–190 Wairau Road,
Auckland 10, New Zealand

First published in West Germany under the title *Momo* by
K. Thienemanns Verlag. Stuttgart 1973
First English translation published in Great Britain under the title
The Gray Gentlemen by Burke Books Publishing Company Limited 1974
This English translation first published in the United States of America
under the title *Momo* by Doubleday & Company, Inc., 1985
Published in Penguin Books by arrangement with
Doubleday & Company, Inc., 1986

Printed in the United States of America by
R. R. Donnelley & Sons Company, Harrisonburg, Virginia
Set in Baskerville

Twinkle, twinkle, little star,
How I wonder what you are!
Up above the world so high,
Like a diamond in the sky!
JANE TAYLOR (1783–1824)

Contents

PART ONE

Momo and Her Friends

ONE

The Amphitheater

LONG, LONG AGO, when people spoke languages quite different from our own, many fine, big cities already existed in the sunny lands of the world. There were towering palaces inhabited by kings and emperors; there were broad streets, narrow alleyways, and winding lanes; there were sumptuous temples filled with idols of gold and marble; there were busy markets selling wares from all over the world; and there were handsome, spacious squares where people gathered to discuss the latest news and make speeches or listen to them. Last but not least, there were theaters—or, more properly, amphitheaters.

An amphitheater resembled a modern circus, except that it was built entirely of stone. Seats for spectators were arranged in tiers, one above the other, like steps lining the crater of a man-made volcano. Many such buildings were circular, others semicircular, others oval.

Some amphitheaters were as big as football stadiums, others could hold no more than a few hundred people. Some were resplendent with columns and statues, others plain and unadorned. Having no roofs, amphitheaters were open to the sky. This was why, in the more luxurious ones, spectators were shielded from the heat of the sun or from sudden downpours by gold-embroidered awnings suspended above their seats. In simple amphitheaters, mats woven of rushes or straw served the same purpose. In short, people made their amphitheaters as simple or luxurious as they could afford—just as long as they had one, for our ancestors were enthusiastic playgoers.

Whenever they saw exciting or amusing incidents acted out onstage, they felt as if these make-believe happenings were more real, in some mysterious way, than their own humdrum lives, and they loved to feast their eyes and ears on this other kind of reality.

Thousands of years have passed since then. The great cities of long ago lie in ruins, together with their temples and palaces. Wind and rain, heat and cold have worn away and eaten into the stonework. Ruins are all that remain of the amphitheaters, too. Crickets now inhabit their crumbling walls, singing a monotonous song that sounds like the earth breathing in its sleep.

A few of these ancient cities have survived to the present day, however. Life there has changed, of course. People ride around in cars and buses, have telephones and electric lights. But here and there among the modern buildings one can still find a column or two, an archway, a stretch of wall, or even an amphitheater dating from olden times.

It was in a city of this kind that the story of Momo took place.

On the southern outskirts of the city, where the fields began and the houses became shabbier and more tumbledown, the ruins of a small amphitheater lay hidden in a clump of pine trees. It had never been a grand place, even in the old days, just a place of entertainment for poor folk. When Momo arrived on the scene, the ruined amphitheater had been almost forgotten. Its existence was known to a few professors of archaeology, but they took no further interest in it because there was nothing more to be unearthed there. It wasn't an attraction to be compared with others in the city, either, so the few stray tourists or sightseers who visited it from time to time merely clambered around on the grass-grown tiers of seats, made a lot of noise, took a couple of snapshots, and went away again. Then silence returned to the stone arena and the crickets started on the next verse of their interminable, unchanging song.

The strange, round building was really known only to the folk who lived in the immediate neighborhood. They grazed their goats there, their children played ball on what had once been the central stage, and sweethearts would sometimes meet there in the evenings.

One day, however, word went around that someone had moved into the ruins. It was a child—a girl, most likely, though this was hard to say because she wore such funny clothes. The newcomer's name was Momo.

Aside from being rather odd, Momo's personal appearance might well have shocked anyone who set store by looking clean and tidy. She was so small and thin that, with the best will in the world, no one could have told her age. Her unruly mop of jet-black hair looked as if it had never seen a comb or a pair of scissors. She had very big, beautiful eyes as black as her hair and feet of almost the same color, for she nearly always went around barefoot. Although she sometimes wore shoes in the wintertime, the only shoes she had were not a pair, and besides, they were far too big for her. This was because Momo owned nothing apart from what she had found lying around or had been given. Her ankle-length dress was a mass of patches of different colors, and over it she wore a man's jacket, also far too big for her, with the sleeves turned up at the wrist. Momo had decided against cutting them off because she wisely reflected that she was still growing, and goodness only knew if she would ever find another jacket as useful as this one, with all its many pockets.

Beneath the grassy stage of the ruined amphitheater, half choked with rubble, were some underground chambers which could be reached by way of a hole in the outer wall, and this was where Momo had installed herself. One afternoon, a group of men and women from the neighborhood turned up and tried to question her. Momo eyed them apprehensively, fearing that they had come to chase her away, but she soon saw that they meant well. Being poor like herself, they knew how hard life could be.

"So," said one of the men, "you like it here, do you?"

Momo nodded.

"And you want to stay here?"

"Yes, very much."

"Won't you be missed, though?"

"No."

"I mean, shouldn't you go home?"

"This is my home," Momo said promptly.

"But where do you come from?"

Momo gestured vaguely at some undefined spot in the far distance.

"Who are your parents, then?" the man persisted.

Momo looked blankly from him to the others and gave a little shrug. The men and women exchanged glances and sighed.

"There's no need to be scared," the man went on, "we haven't come to throw you out. We'd like to help you, that's all."

Momo nodded and said nothing, not entirely reassured.

"You're called Momo, aren't you?"

"Yes."

"That's a pretty name, but I've never heard it before. Who gave it to you?"

"I did," said Momo.

"You chose your own name?"

"Yes."

"When were you born?"

Momo pondered this. "As far as I can remember," she said at last, "I've always been around."

"But don't you have any aunts or uncles or grandparents? Don't you have any relations at all who'd give you a home?"

Momo just looked at the man in silence for a while. Then she murmured, "This is my home, here."

"That's all very well," said the man, "but you're only a kid. How old are you really?"

Momo hesitated. "A hundred," she said.

They all laughed because they thought she was joking.

"No, seriously, how old are you?"

"A hundred and two," Momo replied, still more hesitantly.

It was some time before the others realized that she'd picked up a few numbers but had no precise idea of their meaning because no one had ever taught her to count.

"Listen," said the man, after conferring with the others, "would you mind if we told the police you're here? Then you'd be put in a children's home where they'd feed you and give you a proper bed and teach you reading and writing and lots of other things. How does that appeal to you?"

Momo gazed at him in horror. "No," she said in a low voice, "I've already been in one of those places. There were other children there, too, and bars over the windows. We were beaten every day for no good reason—it was awful. One night I climbed the wall and ran away. I wouldn't want to go back there."

"I can understand that," said an old man, nodding, and the others could understand and nodded too.

"Very well," said one of the women, "but you're still so little. Someone has to take care of you."

Momo looked relieved. "I can take care of myself."

"Can you really?" said the woman.

Momo didn't answer at once. Then she said softly, "I don't need much."

Again the others exchanged glances and sighed.

"Know something, Momo?" said the man who had spoken first. "We were wondering if you'd like to move in with one of us. It's true we don't have much room ourselves, and most of us already have a horde of children to feed, but we reckon one more won't make any difference. What do you say?''

"Thank you," Momo said, smiling for the first time. "Thank you very much, but couldn't you just let me go on living here?"

After much deliberation, the others finally agreed. It occurred to them that she would be just as well off here as with one of them, so they decided to look after Momo together. It would be easier, in any case, for all of them to do so than for one of them alone.

They made an immediate start by spring-cleaning Momo's dilapidated dungeon and refurbishing it as best they could. One of them, a bricklayer by trade, built her a miniature cooking stove and produced a rusty stovepipe to go with it. The old man, who was a carpenter, nailed together a little table and two chairs out of some packing cases. As for the womenfolk, they brought along a decrepit iron bedstead adorned with curlicues, a mattress with only a few rents in it, and a couple of blankets. The stone cell beneath the stage of the ruined amphitheater became a snug little room. The bricklayer, who fancied himself as an artist, added the finishing touch by painting a pretty flower picture on the wall. He even painted a pretend frame around it and a pretend nail as well.

Last of all, the people's children came along with whatever food they could spare. One brought a morsel of cheese, another a hunk of bread, another some fruit, and so on. And because so many children came, the occasion turned into a regular housewarming party. Momo's installation in the old amphitheater was celebrated as zestfully as only the poor of this world know how.

And that was the beginning of her friendship with the people of the neighborhood.

TWO

Listening

MOMO WAS COMFORTABLY OFF from now on, at least in her own estimation. She always had something to eat, sometimes more and sometimes less, depending on circumstances and on what people could spare. She had a roof over her head, she had a bed to sleep in, and she could make herself a fire when it was cold. Most important of all, she had acquired a host of good friends.

You may think that Momo had simply been fortunate to come across such friendly people. This was precisely what Momo herself thought, but it soon dawned on her neighbors that they had been no less fortunate. The girl became so important to them, they wondered how they had ever managed without her in the past. And the longer she stayed with them, the more indispensable she became—so indispensable, in fact, that their one fear was that she might someday move on.

The result was that Momo received a stream of visitors. She was almost always to be seen with someone sitting beside her, talking earnestly, and those who needed her but couldn't come themselves would send for her instead. As for those who needed her but hadn't yet realized it, the others used to tell them, "Why not go and see Momo?"

In time, these words became a stock phrase with the local inhabitants. Just as they said, "All the best!" or "So long!" or "Heaven only knows!," so they took to saying, on all sorts of occasions, "Why not go and see Momo?"

Was Momo so incredibly smart that she always gave good advice, or found the right words to console people in need of consolation, or delivered fair and farsighted opinions on their problems?

No, she was no more capable of these things than anyone else her age.

So could she do things that put people in a good mood? Could she sing like a bird or play an instrument? Given that she lived in a kind of circus, could she dance or do acrobatics?

No, it wasn't any of these either.

Was she a witch, then? Did she know some magic spell that would drive away troubles and cares? Could she read a person's palm or foretell the future in some other way?

No, what Momo was better at than anyone else was *listening*.

Anyone can listen, you may say—what's so special about that?—but you'd be wrong. Very few people know how to listen properly, and Momo's way of listening was quite unique.

She listened in a way that made slow-witted people have flashes of inspiration. It wasn't that she actually said anything or asked questions that put such ideas into their heads. She simply sat there and listened with the utmost attention and sympathy, fixing them with her big, dark eyes, and they suddenly became aware of ideas whose existence they had never suspected.

Momo could listen in such a way that worried and indecisive people knew their own minds from one moment to the next, or shy people felt suddenly confident and at ease, or downhearted people felt happy and hopeful. And if someone felt that his life had been an utter failure, and that he himself was only one among millions of wholly unimportant people who could be replaced as easily as broken windowpanes, he would go and pour out his heart to Momo. And, even as he spoke, he would come to realize by some mysterious means that he was absolutely wrong: that there was only one person like himself in the whole world, and that, consequently, he mattered to the world in his own particular way.

Such was Momo's talent for listening.

One day, Momo received a visit from two near neighbors who had quarreled violently and weren't on speaking terms. Their friends had urged them to "go and see Momo" because it didn't do for neighbors to live at daggers drawn. After objecting at first, the two men had reluctantly agreed.

One of them was the bricklayer who had built Momo's stove and painted the pretty flower picture on her wall. Salvatore by name, he was a strapping fellow with a black mustache that curled up at the ends. The other, Nino, was skinny and always looked tired. Nino ran a small inn on the outskirts of town, largely patronized by a handful of old men who spent the entire evening reminiscing over one glass of wine. Nino and his plump wife, Liliana, were also friends of Momo's and had often brought her good things to eat.

So there the two men sat, one on each side of the stone arena, silently scowling at nothing in particular.

When Momo saw how angry with each other they were, she couldn't decide which one of them to approach first. Rather than offend either of them, she sat down midway between them on the edge of the arena and looked at each in turn, waiting to see what would happen. Lots of things take time, and time was Momo's only form of wealth.

After the two of them had sat there in silence for minutes on end, Salvatore abruptly stood up. "I'm off," he announced. "I've shown my goodwill by coming here, but the man's as stubborn as a mule, Momo, you can see that for yourself." And he turned on his heel.

"Goodbye and good riddance!" Nino called after him.

"You needn't have bothered to come in the first place. I wouldn't make up with a vicious brute like you."

Salvatore swung around, puce with rage. "Who's a vicious brute?" he demanded menacingly, retracing his steps. "Say that again—if you dare!"

"As often as you like!" yelled Nino. "I suppose you think you're too big and tough for anyone to speak the truth to your face. Well, *I* will—to you and anyone else that cares to listen. That's right, come here and murder me the way you tried to the other day!"

"I wish I had!" roared Salvatore, clenching his fists. "There you are, Momo, you see the dirty lies he tells? All I did was take him by the scruff of the neck and dunk him in the pool of slops behind that lousy inn of his. You couldn't even drown a rat in that." Readdressing himself to Nino, he shouted, "Yes, you're still alive and kicking, worse luck!"

Insults flew thick and fast after that, and for a while Momo was at a loss to know what it was all about and why the pair of them were so furious with each other. It transpired, by degrees, that Salvatore's only reason for assaulting Nino was that Nino had slapped his face in the presence of some customers, though Nino counterclaimed that Salvatore had previously tried to smash all his crockery.

"That's another dirty lie!" Salvatore said angrily. "I only threw a jug at the wall, and that was cracked already."

"Maybe," Nino retorted, "but it was *my* jug. You had no right to do such a thing."

Salvatore protested that he had every right, seeing that Nino had cast aspersions on his professional skill. He turned to Momo. "Know what he said about me? He said I couldn't build a wall straight because I was drunk twenty-four hours a day. My great grandfather was the same, he said, and he'd helped to build the Leaning Tower of Pisa."

"But Salvatore," said Nino, "I was only joking."

"Some joke," growled Salvatore. "Very funny, I don't think!"

It then emerged that Nino had only been paying Salvatore

back for another joke. He'd woken up one morning to find some words daubed on the tavern door in bright red paint. They read: THIS INN IS OUT. Nino had found that just as unamusing.

The two of them spent some time wrangling over whose had been the better joke. Then, after working themselves up into a lather again, they broke off.

Momo was staring at them wide-eyed, but neither man quite knew how to interpret her gaze. Was she secretly laughing at them, or was she sad? Although her expression gave no clue, they suddenly seemed to see themselves mirrored in her eyes and began to feel sheepish.

"Okay," said Salvatore, "maybe I shouldn't have painted those words on your door, Nino, but I wouldn't have done it if you hadn't refused to serve me so much as a single glass of wine. That was against the law, as you know full well. I've always paid up, and you'd no call to treat me that way."

"Oh, hadn't I just!" Nino retorted. "What about the St. Anthony business? Ah, that's floored you, hasn't it! You cheated me right, left, and center, and I wasn't going to take it lying down."

"*I* cheated *you?*" Salvatore protested, smiting his brow. "You've got it the wrong way around. It was *you* that tried to cheat *me,* but you didn't succeed."

The fact was, Nino had hung a picture of St. Anthony on the wall of the barroom—a clipping from an illustrated magazine which he had cut out and framed. Salvatore offered to buy this picture one day, ostensibly because he found it so beautiful. By dint of skillful haggling, Nino had persuaded Salvatore to part with a radio in exchange, laughing up his sleeve to think that Salvatore was getting the worst of the bargain.

After the deal had been struck, it turned out that tucked between the picture and its cardboard backing was a bank note of which Nino had known nothing. Discovering that *he* had been outsmarted, Nino angrily demanded the money back because it hadn't been included in the bargain. Salvatore refused to hand it over, whereupon Nino refused to serve him anymore, and that was how it had all begun.

Once they had traced their vendetta back to its original cause, the men fell silent for a while.

Then Nino said, "Be honest, Salvatore, did you or didn't you know about that money before we made the deal?"

"Of course I knew, or I wouldn't have gone through with it."

"In other words, you diddled me."

"What? You mean you really didn't know about the money?"

"No, I swear I didn't."

"There you are, then! It was you that tried to diddle me, or you wouldn't have taken my radio in exchange for a worthless scrap of newsprint."

"How did *you* know about the money?"

"I saw another customer tuck it into the back as a thank-you to St. Anthony, a couple of nights before."

Nino chewed his lip. "Was it a lot of money?"

"Only what my radio was worth," said Salvatore.

"I see," Nino said thoughtfully. "So that's what all this is about—a clipping from a magazine."

Salvatore scratched his head. "I guess so," he growled. "You're welcome to have it back, Nino."

"Certainly not," Nino replied with dignity. "A deal's a deal. We shook hands on it, after all."

Quite suddenly, they both burst out laughing. Clambering down the stone steps, they met in the middle of the grassy arena, exchanged bear hugs, and slapped each other on the back. Then they hugged Momo and thanked her profusely.

When they left a few minutes later, Momo stood waving till they were out of sight. She was glad her two friends had made up.

Another time, a little boy brought her his canary because it wouldn't sing. Momo found that a far harder proposition. She

had to sit and listen to the bird for a whole week before it
started to trill and warble again.

Momo listened to everyone and everything, to dogs and
cats, crickets and tortoises—even to the rain and the wind in

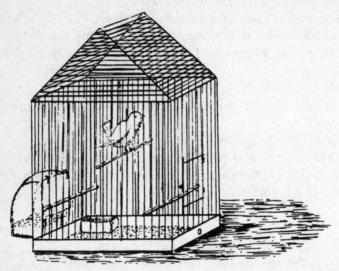

the pine trees—and all of them spoke to her after their own
fashion.

Many were the evenings when, after her friends had gone
home, she would sit by herself in the middle of the old stone
amphitheater, with the sky's starry vault overhead, and simply
listen to the great silence around her.

Whenever she did this, she felt she was sitting at the center
of a giant ear, listening to the world of the stars, and she
seemed to hear soft but majestic music that touched her heart
in the strangest way. On nights like these, she always had the
most beautiful dreams.

Those who still think that listening isn't an art should see if
they can do half as well.

THREE

Make-believe

ALTHOUGH MOMO LISTENED to grown-ups and children with equal sympathy and attention, the children had a special reason for enjoying their visits to the amphitheater as much as they did. Now that she was living there, they found they could play better games than ever before. They were never bored for an instant, but not because she contributed a lot of ingenious suggestions. Momo was there and joined in, that was all, but for some reason her mere presence put bright ideas into their heads. They invented new games every day, and each was an improvement on the last.

One hot and sultry afternoon, a dozen or so children were sitting around on the stone steps waiting for Momo, who had gone for a stroll nearby, as she sometimes did. From the look of the sky, which was filled with fat, black clouds, there would soon be a thunderstorm.

"I'm going home," said one girl, who had a little sister with her. "Thunder and lightning scares me."

"What about when you're at home?" asked a boy wearing glasses. "Doesn't it scare you there?"

"Of course it does," she said.

"Then you may as well stay," said the boy.

The girl shrugged her shoulders and nodded. After a while she said, "But maybe Momo won't turn up."

"So what?" another voice broke in. It belonged to a rather ragged and neglected-looking boy. "Even if she doesn't, we can still play a game."

"All right, but what?"

"I don't know. Something or other."

"Something or other's no good. Anyone got an idea?"

"I know," said a fat boy with a high-pitched voice. "Let's pretend the amphitheater's a ship, and we sail off across uncharted seas and have adventures. I'll be the captain, you can be first mate, and you can be a professor—a scientist, because it's a scientific expedition. The rest of you can be sailors."

"What about us girls?" came a plaintive chorus. "What'll we be?"

"Girl sailors. It's a ship of the future."

The fat boy's idea sounded promising. They tried it out, but everyone started squabbling and the game never got underway. Before long they were all sitting around on the steps again, waiting.

Then Momo turned up, and everything changed.

The *Argo*'s bow rose and fell, rose and fell, as she swiftly but steadily steamed through the swell toward the South Coral Sea. No ship in living memory had ever dared to sail these perilous waters, which abounded with shoals, reefs, and mysterious sea monsters. Most deadly of all was the so-called Traveling Tornado, a waterspout that forever roamed this sea like some cunning beast of prey. The waterspout's route was quite unpredictable, and any ship caught up in its mighty embrace was promptly reduced to matchwood.

Being a research vessel, of course, the *Argo* had been specially designed to tackle the Traveling Tornado. Her hull was

entirely constructed of adamantium, a steel as tough and flex-
ible as a sword blade, and had been cast in one piece by a
special process that dispensed with rivets and welded seams.

For all that, few captains and crews would have had the
courage to face such incredible hazards. Captain Gordon of
the *Argo* had that courage. He gazed down proudly from the
bridge at the men and women of his crew, all of whom were
experts in their particular field. Beside him stood his first
mate, Jim Ironside, an old salt who had already survived a
hundred and twenty-seven hurricanes.

Stationed on the sun deck farther aft were Professor Eisenstein, the expedition's senior scientist, and his assistants
Moira and Sarah, who had as much information stored in their
prodigious memories as a whole reference library. All three
were hunched over their precision instruments, quietly conferring in complicated scientific jargon.

Seated cross-legged a little apart from them was Momosan,
a beautiful native girl. Now and again the professor would
consult her about some special characteristic of the South
Coral Sea, and she would reply in her melodious Hula dialect,
which he alone could understand.

The purpose of the expedition was to discover what caused
the Traveling Tornado and, if possible, make the sea safe for
other ships by putting an end to it. So far, however, there had
been no sign of the tornado and all was quiet.

Quite suddenly, the captain's thoughts were interrupted by
a shout from the lookout in the crow's nest. "Captain!" he
called down, cupping his hands around his mouth. "Unless
I'm crazy, there's a glass island dead ahead of us!"

The captain and Jim Ironside promptly leveled their
telescopes. Professor Eisenstein and his two assistants hurried up, bursting with curiosity, but the beautiful native girl
calmly remained seated. The peculiar customs of her tribe
forbade her to seem inquisitive.

When they reached the glass island, as they very soon did,
the professor scrambled down a rope ladder and gingerly

stepped ashore. The surface was not only transparent but so slippery that he found it hard to keep his footing.

The island was circular and about fifty feet across, with a sort of dome in the center. On reaching the summit, the professor could distinctly make out a light flashing deep in the heart of the island. He passed this information to the others, who were eagerly lining the ship's rail.

"From what you say," said Moira, "it must be a *Blancmangius viscosus.*"

"Perhaps," Sarah chimed in, "though it could equally be a *Jellybeania multicolorata.*"

Professor Eisenstein straightened up and adjusted his glasses. "In my opinion," he said, "we're dealing with a variety of the common *Chocolatus indigestibilis,* but we can't be sure till we've examined it from below."

The words were scarcely out of his mouth when three girl sailors, all of whom were world-famous scuba divers and had already pulled on their wet suits, plunged over the side and vanished into the blue depths.

Nothing could be seen for a while but air bubbles. Then one of the girls, Sandra, shot to the surface. "It's a giant jellyfish!" she gasped. "The other two are caught up in its tentacles and can't break loose. We must save them before it's too late!" So saying, she disappeared again.

Without hesitation, a hundred frogmen led by Commander Franco, nicknamed "the Dolphin" because of his skill and experience, dived into the sea. A tremendous battle raged beneath the surface, which soon became covered with foam, but the gigantic creature's strength was such that not even a hundred brave men could release the girls from its terrible embrace.

The professor turned to his assistants with a puzzled frown. "Something in these waters seems conducive to the growth of abnormally large sea creatures," he observed. "What an interesting phenomenon!"

Meanwhile, Captain Gordon and his first mate had come to a decision.

"Back!" shouted Jim Ironside. "All hands back on board! We'll have to slice the monster in half—it's the girls' only hope."

"Dolphin" Franco and his frogmen climbed back on board. After going astern for a short distance, the *Argo* headed straight for the jellyfish at maximum speed. The steel ship's bow was as sharp as a razor. Without a sound—almost without a jolt—it sliced the huge creature in half. Although this maneuver was fraught with danger for the girls entangled in its tentacles, Jim Ironside had gauged his course to within a hair's breadth and steered right between them. Instantly, the tentacles on each half of the jellyfish went limp and lifeless, and the trapped girls managed to extricate themselves.

They were welcomed back on board with joy. Professor Eisenstein hurried over to them. "It was all my fault," he said. "I should never have sent you down there. Forgive me for risking your lives like that."

"There's nothing to forgive, Professor," one of the girls replied with a carefree laugh. "It's what we came for, after all."

"Danger's our trade," the other girl put in.

But there was no time to say more. Because of the rescue operation, the captain and his crew had completely forgotten to keep watch on the sea. Only now, in the nick of time, did they become aware that the Traveling Tornado had appeared on the horizon and was racing toward them.

An immense roller tossed the *Argo* into the air, hurled her onto her side, and sent her plummeting into a watery abyss. Any crew less courageous and experienced than the *Argo*'s would have been washed overboard or paralyzed with fear by this very first onslaught, but Captain Gordon stood four-square on his bridge as though nothing had happened, and his sailors were just as unperturbed. Momosan, the beautiful native girl, being unaccustomed to such storm-tossed seas, was the only person to take refuge in a lifeboat.

The whole sky turned pitch-black within seconds. Shrieking and roaring, the tornado flung itself at the *Argo,* alternately catapulting her sky-high and sucking her down into cavernous troughs. Its fury seemed to grow with every passing minute as it strove in vain to crush the ship's steel hull.

The captain calmly gave orders to the first mate, who passed them on to the crew in a stentorian voice. Everyone remained at his or her post. Professor Eisenstein and his assistants, far from abandoning their scientific instruments, used them to estimate where the eye of the storm must be, for that was the course to steer. Captain Gordon secretly marveled at the composure of these scientists, who were not, after all, as closely acquainted with the sea as himself and his crew.

A shaft of lightning zigzagged down and struck the ship's hull, electrifying it from stem to stern. Sparks flew whenever the crew touched anything, but none of them worried. Everyone on board had spent months training hard for just such an emergency. The only trouble was, the thinner parts of the ship—cables and stanchions, for instance—began to glow like the filament in an electric light bulb, and this made the crew's work harder despite the rubber gloves they were wearing.

Fortunately, the glow was soon extinguished by a downpour heavier than anyone on board, with the exception of Jim Ironside, had ever experienced. There was no room for any air between the raindrops—they were too close together—so they all had to put on masks and breathing apparatus.

Flashes of lightning and peals of thunder followed one another in quick succession, the wind howled, and mast-high breakers deluged everything with foam. With all engines running full ahead, the *Argo* inched her way forward against the elemental might of the storm. Down below in the boiler rooms, engineers and stokers made superhuman efforts. They had lashed themselves in place with stout ropes so that the ship's violent pitching and tossing would not hurl them into the open furnaces.

But when, at long last, the *Argo* and her crew reached the innermost eye of the storm, what a sight confronted them!

Gyrating on the surface of the sea, which had been ironed flat as a pancake by the sheer force of the storm, was a huge figure. Seemingly poised on one leg, it grew wider the higher one looked, like a mountainous humming top rotating too fast for the eye to make it out in any detail.

"A *Teetotum elasticum!*" the professor exclaimed gleefully, holding on to his glasses to prevent them from being washed off his nose by the rain.

"Maybe you'd care to translate that," growled Jim Ironside. "We're only simple seafaring folk, and—"

"Don't bother the professor now," Sarah broke in, "or you'll ruin a unique opportunity. This spinning-top creature probably dates from the earliest phase of life on earth—it must be over a billion years old. The one variety known today is so small you can only see it under a microscope. It's sometimes found in tomato ketchup, or, even more rarely, in chewing gum. A specimen as big as this may well be the only one in existence."

"But we're here to eliminate it," said the captain, shouting to make himself heard above the sound of the storm. "All right, Professor, tell us how to stop that infernal thing."

"Your guess is as good as mine," the professor replied. "We scientists have never had a chance to study it."

"Very well," said the captain. "We'll try a few shots at it and see what happens."

"What a shame," the professor said sadly. "Fancy shooting the sole surviving specimen of a *Teetotum elasticum!*"

But the antifriction gun had already been trained on the giant spinning top.

"Fire!" ordered the captain.

The twin barrels emitted a tongue of flame a mile long. There was no bang, of course, because an antifriction gun, as everyone knows, bombards its target with proteins.

The flaming missiles streaked toward the *Teetotum* but were caught and deflected. They circled the huge figure a few times, traveling ever faster, ever higher, until they disappeared into the black clouds overhead.

"It's no use," Captain Gordon shouted. "We'll simply have to get closer."

"We can't, sir," Jim Ironside shouted back. "The engines are already running full ahead, and that's only just enough to keep us from being blown astern."

"Any suggestions, Professor?" the captain asked, but Professor Eisenstein merely shrugged. His assistants were equally devoid of ideas. It looked as if the expedition would have to be abandoned as a failure.

Just then, someone tugged at the professor's sleeve. It was Momosan, the beautiful native girl.

"*Malumba,*" she said, gesturing gracefully. "*Malumba oisitu sono. Erweini samba insaltu lolobindra. Kramuna heu beni beni sado-gau.*"

The professor raised his eyebrows. "*Babalu?*" he said inquiringly. "*Didi maha feinosi intu ge doinen malumba?*"

The beautiful native girl nodded eagerly. "*Dodo um aufa shulamat va vada,*" she replied.

"*Oi oi,*" said the professor, thoughtfully stroking his chin.

"What does she say?" asked the first mate.

"She says," explained the professor, "that her tribe has a very ancient song that would send the Traveling Tornado to sleep—or would, if anyone were brave enough to sing it to the creature."

"Don't make me laugh!" growled Jim Ironside. "Who ever heard of singing a tornado to sleep?"

"What do you think, Professor?" asked Sarah. "Is it scientifically feasible?"

"One should always try to keep an open mind," said the professor. "Many of these native traditions contain a grain of truth. The *Teetotum elasticum* may be sensitive to certain sonic vibrations. We simply know too little about its mode of existence."

"It can't do any harm," the captain said firmly, "so let's give it a try. Tell her to carry on."

The professor turned to Momosan and said, "*Malumba didi oisafal huna huna, vavadu?*"

She nodded and began to sing a most peculiar song. It consisted of a handful of notes repeated over and over again:

"Eni meni allubeni,
vanna tai susura teni."

As she sang, she clapped her hands and pranced around in time to the refrain.

The tune and the words were so easy to remember that the rest joined in, one after another, until the entire crew was singing, clapping, and cavorting around in time to the music. Nothing could have been more astonishing than to see the professor himself and that old sea dog, Jim Ironside, singing and clapping like children in a playground.

And then, lo and behold, the thing they never thought would happen came to pass: the Traveling Tornado rotated more and more slowly until it came to a stop and began to sink beneath the waves. With a thunderous roar, the sea closed over it. The storm died away, the rain ceased, the sky became blue and cloudless, the waves subsided. The *Argo* lay motionless on the glittering surface as if nothing but peace and tranquillity had ever reigned there.

"Members of the crew," said Captain Gordon, with an appreciative glance at each in turn, "we pulled it off!" The captain never wasted words, they all knew, so they were doubly delighted when he added, "I'm proud of you."

"I think it must really have been raining," said the girl who had brought her little sister along. "I'm soaked, that's for sure."

She was right. The real storm had broken and moved on, and no one was more surprised than she to find that she had completely forgotten to be scared of the thunder and lightning while sailing aboard the *Argo*.

The children spent some time discussing their adventurous voyage and swapping personal experiences. Then they said goodbye and went home to dry off.

The only person slightly dissatisfied with the outcome of the game was the boy who wore glasses. Before leaving, he

said to Momo, "I still think it was a shame to sink the *Teetotum elasticum,* just like that. The last surviving specimen of its kind, imagine! I do wish I could have taken a closer look at it."

But on one point they were all agreed: the games they played with Momo were more fun than any others.

FOUR

Two Special Friends

EVEN WHEN PEOPLE have a great many friends, there are always one or two whom they love best of all, and Momo was no exception.

She had two very special friends who came to see her every day and shared what little they had with her. One was young and the other old, and Momo could not have said which of them she loved more.

The old one's name was Beppo Roadsweeper. Although he must have had a proper surname, everyone including Beppo himself used the nickname that described his job, which was sweeping roads.

Beppo lived near the amphitheater in a homemade shack built of bricks, corrugated iron, and tar paper. He was not much taller than Momo, being an exceptionally small man and bent-backed into the bargain. He always kept his head cocked to one side—it was big, with a single tuft of white hair on top—and wore a diminutive pair of steel-rimmed spectacles on his nose.

Beppo was widely believed to be not quite right in the head. This was because, when asked a question, he would give an amiable smile and say nothing. If, after pondering the question, he felt it needed no answer, he still said nothing. If it did, he would ponder what answer to give. He could take as long as a couple of hours to reply, or even a whole day. By this time the person who had asked the question would have forgotten what it was, so Beppo's answer seemed peculiar in the extreme.

Only Momo was capable of waiting patiently enough to grasp his meaning. She knew that Beppo took as long as he did because he was determined never to say anything untrue. In his opinion, all the world's misfortunes stemmed from the countless untruths, both deliberate and unintentional, which people told because of haste or carelessness.

Every morning, long before daybreak, Beppo rode his squeaky old bicycle to a big depot in town. There, he and his fellow roadsweepers waited in the yard to be issued brooms and pushcarts and told which streets to sweep. Beppo enjoyed these hours before dawn, when the city was still asleep, and he did his work willingly and well. It was a useful job, and he knew it.

He swept his allotted streets slowly but steadily, drawing a deep breath before every step and every stroke of the broom. Step, breathe, sweep, breathe, step, breathe, sweep. . . . Every so often he would pause awhile, staring thoughtfully into the distance. And then he would begin again: step, breathe, sweep. . . .

While progressing in this way, with a dirty street ahead of him and a clean one behind, he often had grand ideas. They were ideas that couldn't easily be put into words, though— ideas as hard to define as a half-remembered scent or a color seen in a dream. When sitting with Momo after work, he would tell her his grand ideas, and her special way of listening would loosen his tongue and bring the right words to his lips.

"You see, Momo," he told her one day, "it's like this. Sometimes, when you've a very long street ahead of you, you think how terribly long it is and feel sure you'll never get it swept."

He gazed silently into space before continuing. "And then you start to hurry," he went on. "You work faster and faster, and every time you look up there seems to be just as much left to sweep as before, and you try even harder, and you panic, and in the end you're out of breath and have to stop—and still the street stretches away in front of you. That's not the way to do it."

He pondered awhile. Then he said, "You must never think of the whole street at once, understand? You must only concentrate on the next step, the next breath, the next stroke of the broom, and the next, and the next. Nothing else."

Again he paused for thought before adding, "That way you enjoy your work, which is important, because then you make a good job of it. And that's how it ought to be."

There was another long silence. At last he went on. "And all at once, before you know it, you find you've swept the whole street clean, bit by bit. What's more, you aren't out of breath." He nodded to himself. "That's important, too," he concluded.

Another time, when he came and sat down beside Momo, she could tell from his silence that he was thinking hard and had something very special to tell her. Suddenly he looked her in the eye and said, "I recognized us." It was a long time before he spoke again. Then he said softly, "It happens sometimes—at midday, when everything's asleep in the heat of the sun. The world goes transparent, like river water, if you know what I mean. You can see the bottom."

He nodded and relapsed into silence. Then he said, even more softly, "There are other times, other ages, down there on the bottom."

He pondered again for a long time, searching for the right words. They seemed to elude him, because he suddenly said, in a perfectly normal tone of voice, "I was sweeping alongside the old city wall today. There are five different-colored stones in it. They're arranged like this, see?"

He drew a big T in the dust with his forefinger and looked at it with his head to one side. All at once he whispered, "I recognized them—the stones, I mean."

After yet another long silence, he went on haltingly, "They're stones from olden times, when the wall was first built. Many hands helped to build the wall, but those stones were put there by two particular people. They were meant as a sign, you see? I recognized it."

Beppo rubbed his eyes. The next time he spoke, it was with something of an effort. "They looked quite different then, those two. Quite different." His concluding words sounded almost defiant. "I recognized them, though," he said. "They were you and me—I recognized us!"

People could hardly be blamed for smiling when they heard Beppo Roadsweeper say such things. Many of them used to point at their heads behind his back, but Momo loved him and treasured every word he uttered.

Momo's other special friend was not only young but the exact opposite of Beppo in every respect. A handsome youth with dreamy eyes and an incredible gift of the gab, he was always playing practical jokes and had such a carefree, infectious laugh that people couldn't help joining in. His first name was Girolamo, but everyone called him Guido.

Like Beppo, Guido took his surname from his job, though he didn't have a proper job at all. One of his many unofficial activities was showing tourists around the city, so he was universally known as Guido Guide. His sole qualification for the job was a peaked cap, which he promptly clapped on his head whenever any tourists strayed into the neighborhood. Then, wearing his most earnest expression, he would march up and offer to show them the sights. If they were rash enough to accept, Guido let fly. He bombarded his unfortunate listeners with such a multitude of made-up names, dates, and historical events that their heads started spinning. Some of them saw through him and walked off in a huff, but the majority took his tales at face value and dropped a few coins into his cap when he handed it around at the end of a sightseeing tour.

Although Guido's neighbors used to chuckle at his flights of fancy, they sometimes looked stern and remarked that it wasn't really right to take good money for dreaming up a pack of lies.

"I'm only doing what poets do," Guido would argue. "Anyway, my customers get their money's worth, don't they? I give them exactly what they want. Maybe you won't find my stories in any guide book, but what's the difference? Who knows if the stuff in the guide books isn't made up too, only no one remembers anymore. Besides, what do you mean by true and untrue? Who can be sure what happened here a thousand or two thousand years ago? Can *you*?"

The others admitted they couldn't.

"There you are, then!" Guido cried triumphantly. "How can you call my stories untrue? Things may have happened just the way I say they did, in which case I've been telling the gospel truth."

It was hard to counter an argument like that, especially when you were up against a fast talker like Guido.

Unfortunately for him, however, not many tourists wanted to see the amphitheater, so he often had to turn his hand to other jobs. When occasion arose he would act as park keeper, dog walker, deliverer of love letters, mourner at funerals, witness at weddings, souvenir seller, cat's meat man, and many other things besides.

But Guido dreamed of becoming rich and famous someday. He planned to live in a fabulously beautiful mansion set in spacious grounds, eat off gold plates, and sleep between silken sheets. He pictured himself as resplendent in his future fame as a kind of sun, and the rays of that sun already warmed him in his poverty—from afar, as it were.

"I'll do it, too," he would exclaim when other people scoffed at his dreams. "You mark my words!"

Quite how he was going to do it, not even he could have

told them, for Guido held a low opinion of perseverance and hard work.

"What's so smart about working hard?" he said to Momo. "Anyone can get rich quick that way, but who wants to look like the people who've sold themselves body and soul for money's sake? Well, they can count me out. Even if there *are* times when I don't have the price of a cup of coffee, I'm still *me*. Guido's still Guido!"

Although it seemed improbable that two people as dissimilar as Guido Guide and Beppo Roadsweeper, with their different attitudes to life and the world in general, should have become friends, they did. Strangely enough, Beppo was the only person who never chided Guido for his irresponsibility; and, just as strangely, fast-talking Guido was the only person who never poked fun at eccentric old Beppo. This, too, may have had something to do with the way Momo listened to them both.

None of the three suspected that a shadow was soon to fall, not only across their friendship but across the entire neighborhood—an ever-growing shadow that was already enfolding the city in its cold, dark embrace. It advanced day by day like an invading army, silently and surreptitiously, meeting no resistance because no one was really aware of it.

But who exactly were the invaders? Even old Beppo, who saw much that escaped other people, failed to notice the men in gray who busily roamed the city in ever-increasing numbers. It wasn't that they were invisible; you simply saw them without noticing them. They had an uncanny knack of making themselves so inconspicuous that you either overlooked them or forgot ever having seen them. The very fact that they had no need to conceal themselves enabled them to go about their business in utter secrecy. Since nobody noticed them, nobody stopped to wonder where they had come from or, indeed, were still coming from, for their numbers continued to grow with every passing day.

The men in gray drove through the streets in smart gray limousines, haunted every building, frequented every restaurant. From time to time they would jot something down in their little gray notebooks.

They were dressed from head to foot in gray suits the color of a spider's web. Even their faces were gray. They wore gray derbies and smoked small gray cigars, and none of them went anywhere without a steel gray briefcase in his hand.

Guido Guide was as unaware as everyone else that several of these men in gray had reconnoitered the amphitheater, busily writing in their notebooks as they did so.

Momo alone had caught sight of their shadowy figures peering over the edge of the ruined building. They signaled to each other and put their heads together as if conferring. Although she could hear nothing, Momo suddenly shivered as she had never shivered before. She drew her baggy jacket more tightly around her, but it did no good because the chill in the air was no ordinary chill. Then the men in gray disappeared.

Momo heard no soft but majestic music that night, as she so often did, but the next day life went on as usual. She thought no more about her weird visitors, and it wasn't long before she, too, forgot them.

FIVE

Tall Stories

AS TIME WENT BY, Momo became absolutely indispensable to Guido. He developed as deep an affection for the ragged little girl as any footloose, fancy-free young man could have felt for any fellow creature.

Making up stories was his ruling passion, as we have already said, and it was in this very respect that he underwent a change of which he himself was fully aware. In the old days, not all of his stories had turned out well. Either he ran short of ideas and was forced to repeat himself, or he borrowed from some movie he'd seen or some newspaper article he'd read. His stories had plodded along, so to speak, but Momo's friendship had suddenly lent them wings.

Most of all, it was when Momo sat listening to him that his imagination blossomed like a meadow in springtime. Children and grown-ups flocked to hear him. He could now tell stories in episodes spanning days or even weeks, and he never ran out of ideas. He listened to himself as enthralled as his audience, never knowing where his imagination would lead him.

The next time some tourists visited the amphitheater—Momo was sitting on one of the steps nearby—he began as follows:

"Ladies and gentlemen, as I'm sure you all know, the Empress Harmonica waged countless wars in defense of her realm, which was under constant attack by the Goats and Hens.

"Having subdued these barbarian tribes for the umpteenth time, she was so infuriated by their endless troublemaking that she threatened to exterminate them, once and for all, unless their king, Raucous II, made amends by sending her his goldfish.

"At that period, ladies and gentlemen, goldfish were still unknown in these parts, but Empress Harmonica had heard from a traveler that King Raucous owned a small fish which, when fully grown, would turn into solid gold. The empress was determined to get her hands on this rare specimen.

"King Raucous laughed up his sleeve at this. He hid the real goldfish under his bed and sent the empress a young whale in a bejeweled soup tureen.

"The empress, who had imagined goldfish to be smaller, was rather surprised at the creature's size. Never mind, she told herself, the bigger the better—the bigger now, the more gold later on. There wasn't a hint of gold about the fish—not even a glimmer—which worried her until King Raucous's envoy explained that it wouldn't turn into gold until it had stopped growing. Consequently, its growth should not be obstructed in any way. Empress Harmonica pronounced herself satisfied with this explanation.

"The young fish grew bigger every day, consuming vast quantities of food, but Empress Harmonica was a wealthy woman. It was given as much food as it could put away, so it grew big and fat. Before long, the soup tureen became too small for it.

" 'The bigger the better,' said the empress, and had it transferred to her bathtub. Very soon it wouldn't fit into her bathtub either, so it was installed in the imperial swimming pool.

Transferring it to the pool was no mean feat, because it now weighed as much as an ox. When one of the slaves carrying it lost his footing the empress promptly had the wretched man thrown to the lions, for the fish was now the apple of her eye.

"Harmonica spent many hours each day sitting beside the swimming pool, watching the creature grow. All she could think of was the gold it would make, because, as I'm sure you know, she led a very luxurious life and could never have enough gold to meet her needs.

" 'The bigger the better,' she kept repeating to herself. These words were proclaimed a national motto and inscribed in letters of bronze on every public building.

"When even the imperial swimming pool became too cramped, as it eventually did, Harmonica built the edifice whose ruins you see before you, ladies and gentlemen. It was a huge, round aquarium filled to the brim with water, and here the whale could at last stretch out in comfort.

"From now on the empress sat watching the great fish day and night—watching and waiting for the moment when it would turn into gold. She no longer trusted a soul, not even her slaves or relations, and dreaded that the fish might be stolen from her. So here she sat, wasting away with fear and worry, never closing her eyes, forever watching the fish as it blithely splashed around without the least intention of turning into gold.

"Harmonica neglected her affairs of state more and more, which was just what the Goats and Hens had been waiting for. Led by King Raucous, they launched one final invasion and conquered the country in no time. They never encountered a single enemy soldier, and the common folk didn't care one way or the other who ruled them.

"When Empress Harmonica finally heard what had happened, she uttered the well-known words, 'Alas, if only I'd . . .' The rest of the sentence is lost in the mists of time, unfortunately. All we know for sure is that she threw herself into this very aquarium and perished alongside the creature that had blighted her hopes. King Raucous celebrated his victory by ordering the whale to be slaughtered, and the entire population feasted on grilled whale steaks for a week.

"Which only goes to show, ladies and gentlemen, how unwise it is to believe all you're told."

That concluded Guido's lecture. Most of his listeners were profoundly impressed and surveyed the ruined amphitheater with awe. Only one of them was skeptical enough to strike a note of doubt. "When is all this supposed to have happened?" he asked.

"I need hardly remind you," said Guido, who was never at a loss for words, "that Empress Harmonica was a contemporary of the celebrated philosopher Nauseous the Elder."

Understandably reluctant to admit his total ignorance of when the celebrated philosopher Nauseous the Elder had lived, the skeptic merely nodded and said, "Ah yes, of course."

All the other tourists were thoroughly satisfied. Their visit had been well worthwhile, they declared, and no guide had ever presented them with such a graphic and interesting account of ancient times. When Guido modestly held out his peaked cap, they showed themselves correspondingly generous. Even the skeptic dropped a few coins into it.

Guido, incidentally, had never told the same story twice since Momo's arrival on the scene; he would have found that far too boring. When Momo was in the audience a floodgate seemed to open inside him, releasing a torrent of new ideas that bubbled forth without his ever having to think twice.

On the contrary, he often had to restrain himself from going too far, as he did the day his services were enlisted by two elderly American ladies whose blood he curdled with the following tale:

"It is, of course, common knowledge, even in your own fair, freedom-loving land, dear ladies, that the cruel tyrant Marxentius Communis, nicknamed "the Red," resolved to mold the world to fit his own ideas. Try as he might, however, he found that people refused to change their ways and remained much the same as they always had been. Toward the end of his life, Marxentius Communis went mad. The ancient world had no psychiatrists capable of curing such mental disorders, as I'm sure you know, so the tyrant continued to rave unchecked. He eventually took it into his head to leave the existing world to its own devices and create a brand-new world of his own.

"He therefore decreed the construction of a globe exactly the same size as the old one, complete with perfect replicas of everything in it—every building and tree, every mountain, river, and sea. The entire population of the earth was compelled, on pain of death, to assist in this vast project.

"First they built the base on which the huge new globe would rest—and the remains of that base, dear ladies, are what you now see before you.

"Then they started to construct the globe itself, a gigantic sphere as big as the earth. Once this sphere had been completed, it was furnished with perfect copies of everything on earth.

"The sphere used up vast quantities of building materials, of course, and these could be taken only from the earth itself. So the earth got smaller and smaller while the sphere got bigger and bigger.

"By the time the new world was finished, every last little scrap of the old world had been carted away. What was more, the whole of mankind had naturally been obliged to move to the new world because the old one was all used up. When it dawned on Marxentius Communis that, despite all his efforts, everything was just as it had been, he buried his head in his toga and tottered off. Where to, no one knows.

"So you see, ladies, this craterlike depression in the ruins before you used to be the dividing line between the old world and the new. In other words, you must picture everything upside down."

The American dowagers turned pale, and one of them said in a quavering voice, "But what became of Marxentius Communis's world?"

"Why, you're standing on it right now," Guido told her. "Our world, ladies, is his!"

The two old things let out a squawk of terror and took to their heels. This time, Guido held out his cap in vain.

Guido's favorite pastime, though, was telling stories to Momo on her own, with no one else around. They were fairy tales, mostly, because Momo liked those best, and they were about Momo and Guido themselves. Being intended just for the two of them, they sounded quite different from any of the other stories Guido told.

One fine, warm evening the pair of them were sitting quietly, side by side, on the topmost tier of stone steps. The first stars were already twinkling in the sky, and a big, silvery moon was climbing above the dark silhouettes of the pine trees.

"Will you tell me a story?" Momo asked softly.

"All right," said Guido. "What about?"

"Best of all I'd like it to be about us," Momo said.

Guido thought awhile. Then he said, "What shall we call it?"

"How about The Tale of the Magic Mirror?"

Guido nodded thoughtfully. "Sounds promising," he said. "Let's see how it turns out." And he put his arm around Momo and began:

"Once upon a time there was a beautiful princess named Momo, who dressed in silk and satin and lived high above the world on a snow-clad mountaintop, in a palace built of stained glass. She had everything her heart could desire. Nothing but the choicest food and wine ever passed her lips. She reclined on silken cushions and sat on ivory chairs. She had everything, as I say, but she was all alone.

"All the people and things around her—her footmen and ladies-in-waiting, her dogs and cats and birds, even her flowers—were merely reflections.

"The fact was, Princess Momo had a magic mirror, big and round and made of the finest silver. Every day and every night she used to send it out into the world, and the big round mirror soared over land and sea, town and countryside. People who saw it weren't a bit surprised. All they ever said was, 'Ah, there's the moon.'

"Well, every time the magic mirror came back to the princess it would empty out the reflections it had collected on its travels, beautiful and ugly, interesting and dull, as the case might be. The princess picked out the ones she liked best. The others she simply threw into a stream, and quicker than the speed of thought these discarded reflections sped back to their owners along the waterways of the earth. That's why you'll find your own reflection looking at you whenever you bend over a stream or a pool of water.

"I forgot to mention that Princess Momo was immortal. Why? Because she'd never seen her own reflection in the magic mirror, and anyone who saw his own reflection in it became mortal at once. Being well aware of this, Princess Momo took care not to do so. She'd always been quite content to live and play with her many other reflections.

"One day, however, the magic mirror brought her a reflection that appealed to her more than any other. It was the reflection of a young prince. As soon as she saw it, she longed to meet him face-to-face. How was she to set about it, though? She didn't know where he lived or who he was—she didn't even know his name.

"For want of a better idea, she decided to look into the magic mirror after all, thinking that it might carry her own reflection to the prince. There was a chance that he might be looking up at the sky when the mirror floated past and would see her in it. Perhaps he would follow the mirror back to the palace and find her there.

"So she gazed into the mirror, long and hard, and sent it off around the world with her reflection. By so doing, of course, she lost her immortality.

"Before saying what happened to her next, I must tell you something about the prince.

"His name was Girolamo, and he ruled a great kingdom of his own creation. This kingdom was situated neither in the present nor the past, but always one day ahead in the Future, which was why it was called Futuria. Everyone who dwelt there loved and admired the prince.

" 'Your Royal Highness,' the prince's advisers told him one day, 'it's time you got married.'

"The prince had no objection, so Futuria's loveliest young ladies were brought to the palace for him to choose from. They all made themselves look as beautiful as possible, because each of them naturally wanted his choice to fall on her.

"Among them, however, was a wicked fairy who had managed to sneak into the palace. The blood that ran in her veins was green and cold, not red and warm, but nobody noticed this because she had painted her face so skillfully.

"When the Prince of Futuria entered the great, golden throne room, she quickly muttered such a potent spell that poor Girolamo had eyes for no one but her. He found her so incomparably beautiful that he asked her on the spot if she would be his wife.

" 'With pleasure,' hissed the wicked fairy, 'but only on one condition.'

" 'Name it,' the prince said promptly, without a second thought.

" 'Very well,' said the wicked fairy, and she smiled so sweetly that the poor prince's head swam. 'For one whole year, you must never look up at the moon in the sky. If you do, you will instantly lose all your royal possessions. You will forget who you really are and find yourself transported to the land of Presentia, where you will lead the life of a poor, unknown wretch. Do you accept my terms?'

" 'If that's all you ask,' cried Prince Girolamo, 'what could be easier!'

"Meanwhile, Princess Momo had been waiting in vain for the prince to appear, so she resolved to venture out into the world and look for him. She let all her reflections go and, leaving her stained glass palace behind, set off down the snow-clad mountainside in her dainty little slippers. She roamed the world until she came to Presentia, by which time her slippers were worn out and she had to go barefoot, but the magic mirror bearing her reflection continued to soar overhead.

"One night, while Prince Girolamo was sitting on the roof of his golden palace, playing checkers with the fairy whose blood was cold and green, he felt a little drop of moisture on his hand.

" 'Ah,' said the green-blooded fairy, 'it's starting to rain.'

" 'It can't be,' said the prince. 'There isn't a cloud in the sky.'

"And he looked up, straight into the big silver mirror soaring overhead, and saw from Princess Momo's reflection that she was weeping, and that one of her tears had fallen onto his hand. And at that instant he realized that the fairy had tricked him—that she wasn't beautiful at all and had cold, green blood in her veins. His true love, he realized, was Princess Momo.

" 'You've broken your promise,' snapped the green-blooded fairy, scowling so hideously that she looked like a snake, 'and now you must pay the price!'

"And then, while Prince Girolamo sat there as though paralyzed, she reached inside him with her long, green fingers and tied a knot in his heart. Instantly forgetting that he was the Prince of Futuria, he slunk out of his palace like a thief in the night and wandered far and wide till he came to Presentia, where he took the name Guido and lived a life of poverty and obscurity. All he'd brought with him was Princess Momo's reflection from the magic mirror, which was blank from then on.

"By now Princess Momo had abandoned the ragged remains of her silk and satin gown. She wore a patchwork dress and a man's castoff jacket, far too big for her, and was living in an ancient ruin.

"When the two of them met there one fine day, Princess Momo failed to recognize poor, good-for-nothing Guido as the Prince of Futuria. Guido didn't recognize her either, because she no longer looked like a princess, but they became companions in misfortune and a source of consolation to each other.

"One evening when the magic mirror, now blank, was floating across the sky, Guido took out Momo's reflection and showed it to her. Crumpled and faded though it was, the princess immediately recognized it as her own—the one she'd sent soaring around the world. And then, as she peered more closely at the poor wretch beside her, she saw he was the long-sought prince for whose sake she had renounced her immortality.

"She told him the whole story, but Guido sadly shook his head. 'Your words mean nothing to me,' he said. 'There's a knot in my heart, and it stops me remembering.'

"So Princess Momo laid her hand on his breast and untied the knot in his heart with ease, and Prince Girolamo suddenly remembered who he was and where he came from. And he took Princess Momo by the hand and led her far, far away, to the distant land of Futuria."

They both sat silent for a while when Guido had finished. Then Momo asked, "Did they ever get married?"

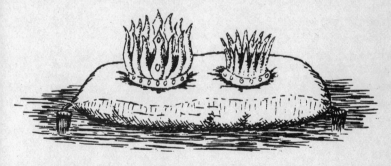

"I think so," said Guido, "—later on."

"And are they dead now?"

"No," Guido said firmly, "I happen to know that for a fact. The magic mirror only made you mortal if you looked into it on your own. If two people looked into it together, it made them immortal again, and that's what those two did."

The big, silver moon floated high above the dark pine trees,

bathing the ruin's ancient stonework in its mysterious light.
Momo and Guido sat there side by side, gazing up at it for a
long time and feeling quite certain that, if only for the space of
that enchanted moment, the pair of them were immortal.

PART TWO

The Men in Gray

SIX

The Timesaving Bank

LIFE HOLDS one great but quite commonplace mystery. Though shared by each of us and known to all, it seldom rates a second thought. That mystery, which most of us take for granted and never think twice about, is time.

Calendars and clocks exist to measure time, but that signifies little because we all know that an hour can seem an eternity or pass in a flash, depending on how we spend it.

Time is life itself, and life resides in the human heart.

The men in gray knew this better than anyone. Nobody knew the value of an hour or a minute, or even of a single second, as well as they. They were experts on time just as leeches are experts on blood, and they acted accordingly.

They had designs on people's time—long-term and well-laid plans of their own. What mattered most to them was that no one should become aware of their activities. They had surreptitiously installed themselves in the city. Now, step-by-step and day-by-day, they were secretly invading its inhabitants' lives and taking them over.

They knew the identity of every person likely to further their plans long before that person had any inkling of it. They waited for the ideal moment to entrap him, and they saw to it that the ideal moment came.

One such person was Mr. Figaro, the barber. Though not by any means a high-class hairdresser, he was well respected in the neighborhood. Neither rich nor poor, he owned a small barbershop in the center of town and employed an apprentice.

One day, Mr. Figaro was standing at the door of his shop waiting for customers. It was the apprentice's day off, so he was alone. Raindrops were spattering the sidewalk and the sky was bleak and dreary—as bleak and dreary as Mr. Figaro's mood.

"Life's passing me by," he told himself, "and what am I getting out of it? Wielding a pair of scissors, chatting to customers, lathering their faces—is that the most I can expect? When I'm dead, it'll be as if I'd never existed."

In fact, Mr. Figaro had no objection at all to chatting. He liked to air his opinions and hear what his customers thought of them. He had no objection to wielding a pair of scissors or lathering faces, either. He genuinely enjoyed his work and knew he did it well. Few barbers could shave the underside of a man's chin as smoothly against the lie of the stubble, but there were times when none of this seemed to matter.

"I'm an utter failure," thought Mr. Figaro. "I mean, what do I amount to? A small-time barber, that's all. If only I could lead the right kind of life, I'd be a different person altogether."

Exactly what form the right kind of life should take, Mr. Figaro wasn't sure. He vaguely pictured it as a distinguished and affluent existence such as he was always reading about in glossy magazines.

"The trouble is," he thought sourly, "my work leaves me no time for that sort of thing, and you need time for the right kind of life. You've got to be free, but I'm a lifelong prisoner of scissors, lather, and chitchat."

At that moment a smart gray limousine pulled up right outside Mr. Figaro's barbershop. A gray-suited man got out and walked in. He deposited his gray briefcase on the ledge in front of the mirror, hung his gray derby on the hat rack, sat down in the barber's chair, produced a gray notebook from his breast pocket, and started leafing through it, puffing meanwhile at a small gray cigar.

Mr. Figaro shut the street door because he suddenly found it strangely chilly in his little shop.

"What's it to be," he asked, "shave or haircut?" Even as he spoke, he cursed himself for being so tactless: the stranger was as bald as an egg.

The man in gray didn't smile. "Neither," he replied in a peculiarly flat and expressionless voice—a gray voice, so to speak. "I'm from the Timesaving Bank. Permit me to introduce myself: Agent No. XYQ/384/b. We hear you wish to open an account with us."

"That's news to me," said Mr. Figaro. "To be honest, I didn't even know such a bank existed."

"Well, you know now," the agent said crisply. He consulted his little gray notebook. "Your name is Figaro, isn't it?"

"Correct," said Mr. Figaro. "That's me."

"Then I've come to the right address," said the man in gray, shutting his notebook with a snap. "You're on our list of applicants."

"How come?" asked Mr. Figaro, who was still at a loss.

"It's like this, my dear sir," said the man in gray. "You're wasting your life cutting hair, lathering faces, and swapping idle chitchat. When you're dead, it'll be as if you'd never existed. If you only had the time to lead the right kind of life, you'd be quite a different person. Time is all you need, right?"

"That's just what I was thinking a moment ago," mumbled Mr. Figaro, and he shivered because it was getting colder and colder in spite of the door being shut.

"You see!" said the man in gray, puffing contentedly at his small cigar. "You need more time, but how are you going to find it? By saving it, of course. You, Mr. Figaro, are wasting time in a totally irresponsible way. Let me prove it to you by simple arithmetic. There are sixty seconds in a minute and sixty minutes in an hour—are you with me so far?"

"Of course," said Mr. Figaro.

Agent No. XYQ/384/b produced a piece of gray chalk and scrawled some figures on the mirror.

"Sixty times sixty is three thousand six hundred, which makes three thousand six hundred seconds in an hour. There are twenty-four hours in a day, so multiply three thousand six hundred by twenty-four to find the number of seconds in a day and you arrive at a figure of eighty-six thousand four hundred. There are three hundred and sixty-five days in a year, as you know, which makes thirty-one million five hundred and thirty-six thousand seconds in a year, or three hundred and fifteen million three hundred and sixty thousand seconds in ten years. How long do you reckon you'll live, Mr. Figaro?"

"Well," stammered Mr. Figaro, thoroughly disconcerted by now, "I hope to live to seventy or eighty, God willing."

"Very well," pursued the man in gray. "Let's call it seventy, to be on the safe side. Multiply three hundred and fifteen million three hundred and sixty thousand by seven and you get a grand total of two billion two hundred and seven million five hundred and twenty thousand seconds." He chalked this figure up on the mirror in outsize numerals—2,207,520,000 —and underlined it several times. "That, Mr. Figaro, is the extent of the capital at your disposal."

Mr. Figaro gulped and wiped his brow, feeling quite dizzy. He'd never realized how rich he was.

"Yes," said the agent, nodding and puffing at his small gray cigar, "it's an impressive figure, isn't it? But let's continue. How old are you now, Mr. Figaro?"

"Forty-two," the barber mumbled. He suddenly felt guilty, as if he'd committed a fraud of some kind.

"And how long do you sleep nights, on average?"

"Around eight hours," Mr. Figaro admitted.

The agent did some lightning calculations. The squeak of

his chalk as it raced across the mirror set Mr. Figaro's teeth on edge.

"Forty-two years at eight hours a night makes four hundred and forty-one million five hundred and four thousand seconds . . . We'll have to write that off, I'm afraid. How much of the day do you devote to work, Mr. Figaro?"

"Another eight hours or so," Mr. Figaro said apologetically.

"Then we'll have to write off the same amount again," the agent pursued relentlessly. "You also spend a certain proportion of the day eating. How many hours would you say, counting all meals?"

"I don't exactly know," Mr. Figaro said nervously. "Two hours, maybe."

"That sounds on the low side to me," said the agent, "but assuming it's correct we get a figure of one hundred and ten million three hundred and seventy-six thousand seconds in forty-two years. To continue: you live alone with your elderly mother, as we know. You spend a good hour with the old woman every day, that's to say, you sit and talk to her although she's so deaf she can scarcely hear a word. That counts as more time wasted—fifty-five million one hundred and eighty-eight thousand seconds, to be precise. You also keep a parrot, a needless extravagance whose demands on your time amount to fifteen minutes a day, or thirteen million seven hundred and ninety-seven thousand seconds in forty-two years."

"B-but—" Mr. Figaro broke in imploringly.

"Don't interrupt!" snapped the agent, his chalk racing faster and faster across the mirror. "Your mother's arthritic as well as deaf, so you have to do most of the housework. You go shopping, clean shoes, and perform other chores of a similar nature. How much time does that consume daily?"

"An hour, maybe, but—"

"So you've already squandered another fifty-five million one hundred and eighty-eight thousand seconds, Mr. Figaro. We also know you go to the movies once a week, sing with a glee club once a week, go drinking twice a week, and spend the rest of your evenings reading or gossiping with friends. In short, you devote some three hours a day to useless pastimes that have lost you another one hundred and sixty-five million five hundred and sixty-four thousand seconds." The agent broke off. "What's the matter, Mr. Figaro, aren't you feeling well?"

"No," said the barber, "—yes, I mean. Please excuse me . . ."

"I'm almost through," said the agent. "First, though, we must touch on a rather personal aspect of your life—your little secret, if you know what I mean."

Mr. Figaro was so cold, his teeth had started to chatter.

"So you know about that too?" he muttered feebly. "I didn't think anyone knew except me and Miss Daria—"

"There's no room for secrets in the world of today," his inquisitor broke in. "Look at the matter rationally and realistically, Mr. Figaro, and answer me one thing: Do you plan to marry Miss Daria?"

"N-no," said Mr. Figaro, "I couldn't do that . . ."

"Quite so," said the man in gray. "Being paralyzed from the waist down, she'll have to spend the rest of her life in a wheelchair, yet you visit her every day for half an hour and take her flowers. Why?"

"She's always so pleased to see me," Mr. Figaro replied, close to tears.

"But looked at objectively, from your own point of view," said the agent, "it's time wasted—twenty-seven million five hundred and ninety-four thousand seconds of it, to date. Furthermore, if we allow for your habit of sitting at the window for a quarter of an hour every night, musing on the day's events, we have to write off yet another thirteen million seven hundred and ninety-seven thousand seconds. Very well, let's see how much time that makes in all."

He drew a line under the long column of figures and added them up with the rapidity of a computer.

The sum on the mirror now looked like this:

Sleep	441,504,000	seconds
Work	441,504,000	"
Meals	110,376,000	"
Mother	55,188,000	"
Parrot	13,797,000	"
Shopping, etc.	55,188,000	"
Friends, glee club, etc.	165,564,000	"
Miss Daria	27,594,000	"
Daydreaming	13,797,000	"
Grand Total	1,324,512,000	seconds

"And that figure," said the man in gray, rapping the mirror with his chalk so sharply that it sounded like a burst of machine-gun fire, "—that figure represents the time you've wasted up to now. What do you say to that, Mr. Figaro?"

Mr. Figaro said nothing. He slumped into a chair in the corner of the shop and mopped his brow with a handkerchief, sweating hard despite the icy atmosphere.

The man in gray nodded gravely. "Yes, you're quite right, my dear sir, you've used up more than half of your original capital. Now let's see how much that leaves of your forty-two years. One year is thirty-one million five hundred and thirty-six thousand seconds, and that, multiplied by forty-two, comes to one billion three hundred and twenty-four million five hundred and twelve thousand seconds."

Beneath the previous total he wrote:

Total time available	1,324,512,000	seconds
Time lost to date	1,324,512,000	"
Balance	0,000,000,000	seconds

Then he pocketed his chalk and waited for the sight of all the zeros to take effect, which they did.

"So that's all my life amounts to," thought Mr. Figaro, absolutely shattered. He was so impressed by the elaborate sum, which had come out perfectly, that he was ready to accept whatever advice the stranger had to offer. It was one of the tricks the men in gray used to dupe prospective customers.

Agent No. XYQ/384/b broke the silence. "Can you really afford to go on like this?" he said blandly. "Wouldn't you prefer to start saving right away, Mr. Figaro?"

Mr. Figaro nodded mutely, blue-lipped with cold.

"For example," came the agent's gray voice in his ear, "if you'd started saving even one hour a day twenty years ago, you'd now have a credit balance of twenty-six million two hundred and eighty thousand seconds. Two hours a day would have saved you twice that amount, of course, or fifty-two million five hundred and sixty thousand. And I ask you, Mr. Figaro, what are two measly little hours in comparison with a sum of that magnitude?"

"Nothing!" cried Mr. Figaro. "A mere fleabite!"

"I'm glad you agree," the agent said smoothly. "And if we calculate how much you could have saved that way after another twenty years, we arrive at the handsome figure of one hundred and five million one hundred and twenty thousand seconds. And the whole of that capital, Mr. Figaro, would have been freely available to you at the age of sixty-two!"

"F-fantastic!" stammered Mr. Figaro, wide-eyed with awe.

"But that's not all," the agent pursued. "The best is yet to come. The Timesaving Bank not only takes care of the time you save, it pays you interest on it as well. In other words, you wind up with more than you put in."

"How much more?" Mr. Figaro asked breathlessly.

"That's up to you," the agent told him. "It depends how much time you save and how long you leave it on deposit with us."

"Leave it on deposit?" said Mr. Figaro. "How do you mean?"

"It's quite simple. If you don't withdraw the time you save for five years, we credit you with the same amount again. Your savings double every five years, do you follow? They're worth four times as much after ten years, eight times as much after fifteen, and so on. Say you'd started saving a mere two hours a day twenty years ago: by your sixty-second birthday, or after forty years in all, you'd have had two hundred and fifty-six times as much in the bank as you originally put in. That would mean a credit balance of twenty-six billion nine hundred and ten million seven hundred and twenty thousand seconds."

And the agent produced his chalk again and wrote the figure on the mirror: 26,910,720,000.

"You can see for yourself, Mr. Figaro," he went on, smiling thinly for the first time. "You'd have accumulated over ten times your entire life span, just by saving a couple of hours a day for forty years. If that's not a paying proposition, I don't know what is."

"You're right," Mr. Figaro said wearily, "it certainly is. What a fool I was not to start saving time years ago! It didn't dawn on me till now, and I have to admit I'm appalled."

"No need to be," the man in gray said soothingly, "—none at all. It's never too late to save time. You can start today, if you want to."

"Of course I want to!" exclaimed Mr. Figaro. "What do I have to do?"

The agent raised his eyebrows. "Surely you know how to save time, my dear sir? Work faster, for instance, and stick to essentials. Spend only fifteen minutes on each customer instead of the usual half hour, and avoid time-wasting conversations. Reduce the hour you spend with your mother by half. Better still, put her in a nice, cheap old folks' home, where someone else can look after her—that'll save you a whole hour a day. Get rid of that useless parrot. See Miss Daria once every two weeks, if at all. Give up your fifteen-minute review of the day's events. Above all, don't squander so much of your precious time on singing, reading, and hobnobbing with your so-called friends. Incidentally, I'd also advise you to hang a really accurate clock on the wall so you can time your apprentice to the nearest minute."

"Fine," said Mr. Figaro. "I can manage all that, but what about the time I save? Do I have to pay it in, and if so where, or should I keep it somewhere safe till you collect it? How does the system operate?"

The man in gray gave another thin-lipped smile. "Don't worry, we'll take care of that. Rest assured, we won't mislay a single second of the time you save. You'll find you haven't any left over."

"All right," Mr. Figaro said dazedly, "I'll take your word for it."

"You can do so with complete confidence, my dear sir." The agent rose to his feet. "And now, permit me to welcome you to the ranks of the great timesaving movement. You're a truly modern and progressive member of the community, Mr. Figaro. I congratulate you." So saying, he picked up his hat and briefcase.

"One moment," said Mr. Figaro. "Shouldn't there be some form of contract? Oughtn't I to sign something? Don't I get a policy of some kind?"

Agent No. XYQ/384/b, who had already reached the door, turned and regarded Mr. Figaro with faint annoyance. "What on earth for?" he demanded. "Timesaving can't be compared with any other kind of saving—it calls for absolute trust on both sides. Your word is good enough for us, especially as you can't go back on it. We'll take care of your savings, though how much you save is entirely up to you—we never bring pressure to bear on our customers. Good day, Mr. Figaro."

On that note, the agent climbed into his smart gray car and purred off.

Mr. Figaro gazed after him, kneading his brow. Although he was gradually becoming warmer again, he felt sick and wretched. The air still reeked of smoke from the agent's cigar, a dense blue haze that was slow to disperse.

Not till the smoke had finally gone did Mr. Figaro begin to feel better. But as it faded, so did the figures chalked up on the mirror, and by the time they had vanished altogether Mr. Figaro's recollection of his visitor had vanished too. He forgot the man in gray but not his new resolution, which he believed to be his alone. The determination to save time now so as to be able to begin a new life sometime in the future had embedded itself in his soul like a poisoned arrow.

When the first customer of the day turned up, Mr. Figaro gave him a surly reception. By doing no more than was absolutely necessary and keeping his mouth shut, he got through in twenty minutes instead of the usual thirty.

From now on he subjected every customer to the same treatment. Although he ceased to enjoy his work, that was of secondary importance. He engaged two assistants in addition to his apprentice and watched them like a hawk to see they didn't waste a moment. Every move they made was geared to a precise timetable, in accordance with the notice that now adorned the wall of the barbershop: TIME SAVED IS TIME DOUBLED!

Mr. Figaro wrote Miss Daria a brief, businesslike note regretting that the pressure of work would prevent him from seeing her in the future. His parrot he sold to a pet shop. As for his mother, he put her in an inexpensive old folks' home and visited her once a month. In the belief that the gray stranger's recommendations were his own decisions, he carried them out to the letter.

Meanwhile, he was becoming increasingly restless and irritable. The odd thing was that, no matter how much time he saved, he never had any to spare; in some mysterious way, it simply vanished. Imperceptibly at first, but then quite unmistakably, his days grew shorter and shorter. Almost before he knew it, another week had gone by, and another month, and another year, and another and another.

Having no recollection of the gray stranger's visit, Mr. Figaro should seriously have asked himself where all his time was going, but that was a question never considered by him or any other timesaver. Something in the nature of a blind obsession had taken hold of him, and when he realized to his horror that his days were flying by faster and faster, as he occasionally did, it only reinforced his grim determination to save time.

Many other inhabitants of the city were similarly afflicted. Every day, more and more people took to saving time, and the more they did so the more they were copied by others—even by those who had no real desire to join in but felt obliged to.

Radio, television, and newspapers daily advertised and extolled the merits of new, timesaving gadgets that would someday leave people free to live the "right" kind of life. Walls and billboards were plastered with posters depicting scenes of happiness and prosperity. Splashed across them in fluorescent lettering were slogans such as:

TIMESAVERS ARE GOING PLACES FAST!
THE FUTURE BELONGS TO TIMESAVERS!
MAKE MORE OF YOUR LIFE—SAVE TIME!

The real picture, however, was very different. Admittedly, timesavers were better dressed than the people who lived near the old amphitheater. They earned more money and had more to spend, but they looked tired, disgruntled, and sour, and there was an unfriendly light in their eyes. They'd never heard the phrase "Why not go and see Momo?" nor did they have anyone to listen to them in a way that would make them reasonable or conciliatory, let alone happy. Even had they known of such a person, they would have been highly unlikely to pay him or her a visit unless the whole affair could be dealt with in five minutes flat, or they would have considered it a waste of time. In their view, even leisure time had to be used to the full, so as to extract the maximum of entertainment and relaxation with the minimum of delay.

Whatever the occasion, whether solemn or joyous, timesavers could no longer celebrate it properly. Daydreaming they regarded almost as a criminal offense. What they could endure least of all, however, was silence, for when silence fell they became terrified by the realization of what was happening to their lives. And so, whenever silence threatened to descend, they made a noise. It wasn't a happy sound, of course, like the hubbub in a children's playground, but an angry, ill-tempered din that grew louder every day.

It had ceased to matter that people should enjoy their work and take pride in it; on the contrary, enjoyment merely slowed them down. All that mattered was to get through as much work as possible in the shortest possible time, so notices to that effect were prominently displayed in every factory and office building. They read:

TIME IS PRECIOUS—DON'T WASTE IT!
or: TIME IS MONEY—SAVE IT!

Similar notices hung above business executives' desks and in boardrooms, in doctors' consulting rooms, shops, restaurants, and department stores—even in schools and kindergartens. No one was left out.

Last but not least, the appearance of the city itself changed more and more. Old buildings were pulled down and replaced with modern ones devoid of all the things that were now thought superfluous. No architect troubled to design houses that suited the people who were to live in them, because that would have meant building a whole range of different houses. It was far cheaper and, above all, more timesaving to make them identical.

Huge modern housing developments sprang up on the city's northern outskirts—endless rows of multistoried tenements as indistinguishable as peas in a pod. And because the buildings all looked alike, so, of course, did the streets. They grew steadily longer, stretching away to the horizon in dead straight lines and turning the countryside into a disciplined desert. The lives of the people who inhabited this desert followed a similar pattern: they ran dead straight for as far as the eye could see. Everything in them was carefully planned and programmed, down to the last move and the last moment of time.

People never seemed to notice that, by saving time, they were losing something else. No one cared to admit that life was becoming ever poorer, bleaker, and more monotonous.

The ones who felt this most keenly were the children, because no one had time for them anymore.

But time is life itself, and life resides in the human heart. And the more people saved, the less they had.

SEVEN

The Visitor

"I DON'T KNOW," Momo said one day. "Seems to me our old friends come here less and less often than they used to. I haven't seen some of them for ages."

She was sitting between Guido Guide and Beppo Road-sweeper on the grass-grown steps of the ruined amphitheater, watching the sun go down.

"Yes," Guido said pensively, "it's the same with me. Fewer and fewer people listen to my stories. It isn't like it used to be. Something's wrong."

"But what?" said Momo.

Guido shrugged, spat on the slate he'd been writing on, and thoughtfully rubbed the letters out. Beppo had found the slate in a garbage can some weeks before and presented it to Momo. It wasn't a new one, of course, and it had a big crack down the middle, but it was quite usable all the same. Guido had been teaching Momo her alphabet ever since. Momo had a very good memory, so she could already read quite well, though her writing was coming on more slowly.

Beppo, who had been pondering Momo's question, nodded and said, "You're right, it's closing in—it's the same all over the city. I've noticed it for quite a time."

"Noticed what?" asked Momo.

Beppo thought awhile. Then he said, "Nothing good." There was another pause before he added, "It's getting cold."

"Never mind," said Guido, putting his arm consolingly around Momo's shoulders, "more and more children come here, anyway."

"Exactly," said Beppo, "that's just it."

"What do you mean?" Momo asked.

Beppo thought for a long time before replying. "They don't come for the sake of our company," he said. "It's a refuge they're after, that's all."

They looked down at the stretch of grass in the middle of the amphitheater, where a newly invented game was in progress. The children included several of Momo's old friends: Paolo, the boy who wore glasses; Maria and her little sister, Rosa; Massimo, the fat boy with the squeaky voice; and Franco, the lad who always looked rather ragged and unkempt. In addition to them, however, there were a number of children who had only been coming for the past few days and one small boy who had first appeared that morning. It looked as if Guido was right; their numbers were increasing every day.

Momo would have been delighted, except that most of the newcomers had no idea how to play. All they did was sit around looking bored and sullen and watching Momo and her friends. Sometimes they deliberately broke up the other children's games and spoiled everything. Squabbles and scuffles were frequent, though these never lasted long because Momo's presence had its usual effect on the newcomers, too, so they soon started having bright ideas themselves and joining in with a will. The trouble was, new children turned up nearly every day, some of them from distant parts of the city, and one spoilsport was enough to ruin a game for everyone else.

But there was another thing Momo couldn't quite understand—a thing that hadn't happened until very recently. More and more often these days, children turned up with all kinds of toys you couldn't really play with: remote-controlled tanks that trundled to and fro but did little else, or space rockets that whizzed around on strings but got nowhere, or model robots that waddled along with eyes flashing and heads swiveling but that was all.

They were highly expensive toys such as Momo's friends had never owned, still less Momo herself. Most noticeable of all, they were so complete, down to the tiniest detail, that they left nothing at all to the imagination. Their owners would spend hours watching them, mesmerized but bored, as they trundled, whizzed, or waddled along. Finally, when that palled, they would go back to the familiar old games in which a couple of cardboard boxes, a torn tablecloth, a molehill, or a handful of pebbles were quite sufficient to conjure up a whole world of make-believe.

For some reason, this evening's game didn't seem to be going too well. The children dropped out, one by one, until they all sat clustered around Guido, Beppo, and Momo. They were hoping for a story from Guido, but that was impossible because the latest arrival had brought along a transistor radio. He was sitting a few feet away with the volume at full blast, listening to commercials.

"Turn it down, can't you?" growled Franco, the shabby-looking lad.

The newcomer pointed to the radio and shook his head. "Can't hear you," he said with an impudent grin.

"Turn it down!" shouted Franco, rising to his feet.

The newcomer paled a little but looked defiant. "Nobody tells *me* what to do," he said. "I can have my radio on as loud as I like."

"He's right," said old Beppo. "We can't forbid him to make such a din, the most we can do is ask him not to."

Franco sat down again. "Then he ought to go someplace else," he grumbled. "He's already ruined the whole afternoon."

"I expect he has his reasons," Beppo said, studying the newcomer intently but not unkindly through his little steel-rimmed spectacles. "He's sure to have."

The newcomer said nothing, but moments later he turned his radio down and looked away.

Momo went over and sat down quietly beside him. He switched off the radio altogether, and for a while all was still.

"Tell us a story, Guido," begged one of the recent arrivals. "Oh yes, do!" the others chimed in. "A funny one—no, an exciting one—no, a fairy tale—no, an adventure story!"

But Guido, for the first time ever, wasn't in the mood for telling stories. At length he said, "I'd far rather you told me something about yourselves and your homes—how you spend your time and why you come here."

The children relapsed into silence. All of a sudden, they looked dejected and uncommunicative.

"We've got a nice new car," one of them said at last. "On Saturdays, when my mother and father have time, they wash it. If I've been good, I'm allowed to help. I want a car like that when I'm older."

"My parents let me go to the movies every day, if I like," said a little girl. "They don't have time to look after me, you see, and it's cheaper than a baby-sitter. That's why I sneak off here and save the money they give me for the movies. When I've saved up enough, I'm going to buy an airplane ticket and go and see the Seven Dwarfs."

"Don't be silly," said another child. "They don't exist."

"They do *so*," retorted the little girl. "I've even seen pictures of them in a travel brochure."

"I've got eleven books on tape," said a little boy, "so I can listen to them whenever I like. Once upon a time my Dad used to tell me stories when he came home from work. That was nice, but he's hardly ever home these days, and even when he is he's too tired and doesn't feel like it."

"What about your mother?" asked Maria.

"She's out all day too."

"It's the same with us," said Maria. "I'm lucky, though,

having Rosa to keep me company." She hugged the little girl on her lap and went on, "When I get home from school I heat up our supper. Then I do my homework, and then"—she shrugged her shoulders—"then we just hang around till it gets dark. We come here, usually."

From the way the children nodded, it was clear that they all fared much the same.

"Personally, I'm glad my parents don't have time for me these days," said Franco, who didn't look glad in the least. "They only quarrel when they're home, and then they take it out on me."

Abruptly, the boy with the transistor looked up and said, "At least I get a lot more pocket money than I used to."

"Sure you do," sneered Paolo. "The grown-ups dish out money to get rid of us. They don't like us anymore—they don't even like themselves. If you ask me, they don't like anything anymore."

"That's not true!" the newcomer exclaimed angrily. "My parents like me a lot. It isn't their fault, not having any time to spare, it's just the way things are. They gave me this transistor to keep me company, and it cost plenty. That proves they're fond of me, doesn't it?"

No one spoke, and suddenly the boy who'd been a spoil-sport all afternoon began to cry. He tried to smother his sobs and wiped his eyes with his grubby fists, but the tears flowed fast, leaving pallid snail tracks in the patches of grime on his cheeks.

The other children gazed at him sympathetically or stared at the ground. They understood him now. Deep down, all of them felt as he did: they felt abandoned.

"Yes," old Beppo repeated after a while, "it's getting cold."

"I may not be able to come here much longer," said Paolo, the boy with glasses.

Momo looked surprised. "Why not?"

"My parents think you're a bunch of lazy good-for-nothings," Paolo explained. "They say you fritter your time away. They say there are too many of your sort around. You've got so much time on your hands, other people have to make do with less and less—that's what they say—and if I keep coming here I'll wind up just like you."

Again there were nods of agreement from the other children, who had been told much the same thing.

Guido looked at each of them in turn. "Is that what *you* think of us too?" he asked. "If so, why do you keep on coming?"

It was Franco who broke the short silence that followed. "I couldn't care less. My old man says I'll end up in prison, anyway. I'm on your side."

"I see," Guido said sadly. "So you *do* think we're stealing time from other people."

The children dropped their eyes and looked embarrassed. At length, gazing intently into Beppo's face, Paolo said, "Our parents wouldn't lie to us, would they?" In a low voice, he added, "Aren't you time-thieves, then?"

At that the old roadsweeper rose to his full but diminutive height, solemnly raised his right hand, and declared, "I have never, never stolen so much as a second of another person's time, so help me God."

"Nor have I," said Momo.

"Nor I," Guido said earnestly.

The children preserved an awed silence. If the three friends had given their solemn word, that was good enough.

"And while we're on the subject," Guido went on, "let me tell you something else. Once upon a time, people used to like coming to see Momo because she listened to them and helped them to know their own minds, if you follow my meaning. Nowadays they seldom stop to wonder *what* they think. They used to enjoy listening to me, too, because my stories helped them to forget their troubles, but they seldom bother with that either. They don't have time for such things, they say, but haven't you noticed something odd? It's strange the things they *don't* have time for anymore."

Guido surveyed the listening children with narrowed eyes and nodded before continuing. "The other day," he said, "I bumped into an old friend in town, a barber by the name of Figaro. We hadn't met for quite a while, and I hardly recognized him, he was so changed—so irritable and grouchy and depressed. He used to be a cheerful type, always singing, always airing his ideas on every subject under the sun. Now, all of a sudden, he hasn't got time for anything like that. The man's just a shadow of his former self—he isn't good old Figaro anymore, if you know what I mean. But now comes the really strange part: if he were the only one, I'd think he'd gone a bit cracked, but he isn't. There are people like Figaro wherever you look—more and more of them every day. Even some of our oldest friends are going the same way. I'm beginning to wonder if it isn't catching."

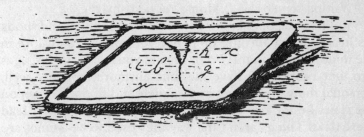

Old Beppo nodded. "You're right," he said, "it must be."

"In that case," said Momo, looking dismayed, "our friends need help."

They spent a long time that evening debating what to do. Of the men in gray and their ceaseless activities, none of them yet had the faintest suspicion.

Momo, who couldn't wait to ask her old friends what was wrong and why they'd stopped coming to see her, spent the next few days looking them up.

The first person she called on was Salvatore, the bricklayer. She knew the house well—Salvatore lived in a little garret under the roof—but he wasn't home. According to the other tenants, he now worked on one of the big new housing developments on the far side of town and was earning a lot of money. He seldom came home at all these days, they said, and when he did it was usually in the small hours. He'd taken to the bottle and was hard to get along with.

Momo decided to wait for him just the same, so she sat down on the stairs outside his door. When it grew dark, she fell asleep.

It must have been long past midnight when she was woken by the sound of unsteady footsteps and raucous singing. Salvatore came blundering upstairs, caught sight of Momo, and stopped short, looking dumbfounded.

"Momo!" he said hoarsely, clearly embarrassed to be seen in his present condition. "So you're still around, eh? What on earth are you doing here?"

"Waiting to see you," Momo replied shyly.

"You're a fine one, I must say!" Salvatore smiled and shook his head. "Fancy turning up to see your old pal Salvatore in the middle of the night! I'd have paid you a visit myself, ages ago, but I just don't have the time anymore, not for—well, personal things." He gestured vaguely and flopped down on the stairs beside her. "You've no idea the kind of life I lead these days. Things aren't the way they used to be—times are changing. Over where I'm working now, everything's done in double-quick time. We all work like fury. One whole floor a day, that's what we have to sling together, day after day. Yes, it isn't like it used to be. Everything's organized—every last move we make . . ."

Momo listened closely as he rambled on, and the longer she listened the less enthusiastic he sounded. Suddenly he lapsed into silence and massaged his face with his work-roughened hands.

"I've been talking rubbish," he said sadly. "I'm drunk again, Momo, that's the trouble. I often get drunk these days, there's no denying it, but that's the only way I can stomach the thought of what we're doing over there. To an honest bricklayer like me, it goes against the grain. Too little cement and too much sand, if you know what that means. Four or five years is all those buildings will last, then they'll collapse if anyone so much as blows his nose. Shoddy workmanship from top to bottom, but that's not the worst of it. Those tenements we're putting up aren't places for people to live in, they're—they're hen coops. It's enough to make you sick. Still, why should I care as long as I get my paycheck at the end of the week? Yes, times are changing all right. It used to give me a kick when we built something worthwhile, but now . . . Someday, when I've made enough money, I'm going to chuck this job and do something different."

He propped his chin on his hands and stared mournfully into space. Momo still said nothing, just went on listening. When Salvatore spoke again, he sounded a little brighter.

"Maybe I should start coming to see you again and telling you my troubles—yes, I really should. What about tomorrow or the day after? I'll have to see if I can fit it in, but I'll come, never fear. Is it a date?"

Momo nodded happily. Then, because they were both very tired, they said good night and she left.

But Salvatore never turned up, neither the next day nor the day after that. He never turned up at all.

The next people Momo called on were Nino the innkeeper and his fat wife Liliana. Their little old tavern, which had damp-stained walls and a vine growing around the door, was on the outskirts of town.

Momo went around to the back, as she used to in the old days. Through the kitchen door, which was open, she could hear Nino and Liliana quarreling violently. Liliana, her plump face shiny with sweat, was clattering pots and pans around on the stove while Nino shouted and gesticulated at her. Their baby was lying in a basketwork crib in the corner, screaming.

Momo sat down quietly beside the baby, took it on her lap, and rocked it gently to and fro until it stopped crying. The grown-ups interrupted their war of words and glanced in her direction.

"Oh, it's you," said Nino, with a ghost of a smile. "Nice to see you again, Momo."

"Hungry?" Liliana inquired rather brusquely.

Momo shook her head.

"So what *do* you want?" Nino demanded. He sounded grumpy. "We're rather pressed for time just now."

"I only wanted to ask why it's been so long since you came to see me," Momo said softly.

Nino frowned. "Search me," he said irritably. "I've got enough worries as it is."

"Yes," snapped Liliana, "he certainly has. Getting rid of our regular customers, that's all he worries about these days. Remember the old men who always used to sit at the corner table in the bar, Momo? Well, he sent them packing—he chucked them out!"

"No, I didn't," Nino protested. "I asked them, quite politely, to take their trade elsewhere. As landlord of this inn, I was perfectly within my rights."

"Your rights, your rights!" Liliana said angrily. "You simply can't act that way—it's mean and cruel. You know they'll never find another inn as easygoing as ours. It wasn't as if they were disturbing anyone."

"There wasn't anyone to disturb, that's why!" retorted Nino. "No decent, well-heeled customers would patronize this place while those stubble-chinned old codgers were lolling in the corner. Besides, there's little enough profit in one measly glass of cheap red wine, which was all they could afford in an evening. We'll never get anywhere at this rate."

Liliana shrugged. "We've done all right so far."

"So far, maybe," Nino said fiercely, "but you know yourself we can't go on like this. They've just raised our rent—I've got to pay 30 percent more than before, and everything's getting more expensive all the time. How am I going to find the money if I turn this place into a home for doddering old down-and-outs? Why should I go easy on other people? No one goes easy on me."

Liliana banged a saucepan down on the stove so hard that the lid rattled. "Let me remind you of something," she said, putting her hands on her mountainous hips. "One of those

doddering old down-and-outs, as you call them, is my Uncle
Enrico, and I won't have you insulting my relations. Enrico's a
decent, respectable man, even if he doesn't have much money
to splash around, like those well-heeled customers you've set
your heart on."

"But Enrico's free to come here any time," Nino said with a
lordly gesture. "I told him he could stay if he wanted, but he
wouldn't."

"Without his cronies? Of course he wouldn't! What did you
expect him to do, sit in a corner by himself?"

"That settles it, then," Nino shouted. "In any case, I've no
intention of ending my days as a two-bit innkeeper, just for
your Uncle Enrico's benefit. I want to get somewhere in life. Is
that such a crime? I aim to make a success of this place, and
not just for my own sake. I'm thinking of you and the baby as
well, Liliana, don't you understand?"

"No, I don't," Liliana said sharply. "If being heartless is the
only way you can get somewhere in life, count me out. I warn
you: sooner or later I'll pack up and leave you, so suit yourself!" On that note, she took the baby from Momo—it had
started crying again—and flounced out of the kitchen.

Nino said nothing for a long time. He lit a cigarette and
twiddled it between his fingers while Momo sat watching him.

"As a matter of fact," he said eventually, "they were nice
old boys—I was fond of them myself. I feel bad about them,
Momo, but what else could I do? Times have changed, you
see." His voice trailed off, and it was a while before he went
on. "Maybe Liliana was right all along. Now that the old men
don't come here anymore, the atmosphere seems strange—
cold, somehow. I don't even like the place myself. I honestly
don't know what to do for the best. Everyone acts the same
way these days, so why should I be the odd man out?" He
hesitated. "Or do you think I should?"

Momo gave an almost imperceptible nod.

Nino caught her eye and nodded too. Then they both
smiled.

"I'm glad you came," Nino said. "I'd quite forgotten the

way we always used to say, 'Why not go and see Momo?' Well, I *will* come and see you again, and I'll bring Liliana with me. The day after tomorrow is our day off. We'll turn up then, all right?"

"All right," said Momo, and went on her way, but not before Nino had presented her with a big bag of apples and oranges.

Sure enough, Nino and Liliana turned up two days later, complete with their baby and a basketful of goodies.

"Just imagine, Momo," said Liliana, beaming, "Nino went to see Uncle Enrico and the other old men. He apologized to them, one after the other, and asked them to come back."

Nino smiled, too, and scratched his ear in some embarrassment. "Yes," he said, "and back they all came. I can say goodbye to my plans for the inn, but at least I like the place again."

He chuckled, and Liliana said, "We'll get by, Nino."

It turned out to be a lovely afternoon, and before leaving they promised to come again soon.

So Momo went the rounds of all her old friends, one by one. She called on the carpenter who had made her little table and chairs out of packing cases, and on the women who had brought her the bedstead. In short, she called on all the people whom she had listened to in the old days, and who, thanks to her, had grown wiser, happier, and more self-assured. Although some of them failed to keep their promise to come and see her, or were unable to for lack of time, so many old faces did turn up that things were almost as they used to be.

Not that Momo knew it, but she was upsetting the plans of the men in gray, and that they couldn't tolerate.

Soon afterward, one exceptionally hot and sultry afternoon, Momo came across a doll on the steps of the old amphitheater.

It wasn't uncommon for children to forget all about expensive toys they couldn't really play with and leave them behind by mistake, but Momo had no recollection of seeing such a doll—and she would certainly have noticed it, because it was a very unusual one.

Nearly as tall as Momo herself, the doll was so lifelike that it might almost have been mistaken for a miniature human being, though not a child or a baby. Its red minidress and high-heeled sandals made it look more like a store window dummy or a stylish young woman about town.

Momo stared at it, fascinated. After a while she put out her hand and touched it. Instantly, the doll blinked a couple of times, opened its rosebud mouth, and said, in a metallic voice that sounded as if it were issuing from a telephone, "Hello, I'm Lola, the Living Doll."

Momo jumped back in alarm. Then, automatically, she replied, "Hello, I'm Momo."

The doll's lips moved again. "I belong to you," it said. "All the other kids envy you because I'm yours."

"You aren't mine," Momo said. "Someone must have left you here by mistake."

She picked the doll up. Again the lips moved. "I'd like some nice new things," said the metallic voice.

"Would you?" Momo thought for a moment. "I doubt if I've got anything you'd care for, but you're welcome to look."

Still holding the doll, Momo clambered through the hole in

the wall that led to her underground room. All her most treasured possessions were in a box beneath the bed. She pulled it out and lifted the lid.

"Here," she said, "this is all I've got. If you'd like anything, just tell me." And she showed the doll a colorful bird's feather, a pebble with pretty streaks in it, a brass button, and a fragment of colored glass. The doll said nothing, so she nudged it.

"Hello," it said. "I'm Lola, the Living Doll."

"I know," said Momo, "but you told me you wanted something. How about this lovely pink seashell? Would you like it?"

"I belong to you," the doll replied. "All the other kids envy you because I'm yours."

"You told me that too," said Momo. "All right, if you don't want any of my things, perhaps we could play a game together. Shall we?"

"I'd like some nice new things," the doll repeated.

"I don't have anything else," Momo said. She took the doll and climbed back outside again. Then she put Lola, the Living Doll, on the ground and sat down facing her.

"Let's pretend you've come to pay me a visit," Momo suggested.

"Hello," said the doll. "I'm Lola, the Living Doll."

"How nice of you to call," Momo replied politely. "Have you come far?"

"I belong to you," the doll said. "All the other kids envy you because I'm yours."

"Look," said Momo, "we'll never get anywhere if you go on repeating yourself like this."

"I'd like some nice new things," said the doll, fluttering its eyelashes.

Momo tried several games in turn, but nothing came of them. If only the doll had remained silent, she could have supplied the answers herself and held an interesting conversation with it. As it was, the very fact that it could talk made conversation impossible.

Before long, Momo was overcome by a sensation so entirely new to her that she took quite a while to recognize it as plain boredom. Although her inclination was to abandon Lola, the Living Doll, and play some other game, she couldn't for some reason tear herself away. So there she sat, gazing at the doll, and the doll, with its glassy blue eyes fixed on hers, gazed back. It was as if they had hypnotized each other.

When, at long last, Momo did manage to drag her eyes away from the doll, she gave a little start of surprise. Parked close by, not that she had heard it drive up, stood a smart gray car. In it sat a man wearing a suit as gray as a spider's web and a stiff, round derby of the same color. He was smoking a small gray cigar, and his face, too, was as gray as ashes.

He must have been watching Momo for some time, because he nodded and smiled at her; and although the day was so hot that the air was dancing in the sunlight, Momo suddenly began to shiver.

The man opened the car door and came over, carrying a steel gray briefcase.

"What a lovely doll you have there," he said in a peculiarly flat and expressionless voice. "It must be the envy of all your playmates."

Momo just shrugged and said nothing.

"I'll bet it cost a fortune," the man in gray went on.

"I wouldn't know," Momo mumbled, feeling rather embarrassed. "I found it lying around."

"Well, I never!" said the man in gray. "You *are* a lucky girl, and no mistake!"

Momo remained silent and hugged her baggy jacket tightly to her. It was growing colder and colder.

"All the same," said the man in gray with a thin-lipped smile, "you don't seem too pleased."

Momo shook her head. She suddenly felt as if happiness had fled the world forever—or rather, as if happiness had never existed and all her ideas of it had been merely figments of her own imagination. At the same time, she had a presentiment of danger.

"I've been watching you for quite a while," pursued the man in gray. "From what I've seen, you don't have the first idea how to play with such a marvelous doll. Shall I show you?"

Momo stared at him in surprise and nodded.

"I'd like some nice new things," the doll squawked suddenly.

"You see?" said the man in gray. "She's actually telling you herself. You can't play with a marvelous doll like this the way you'd play with any old doll, that's obvious. Anyway, it isn't what she's meant for. If you don't want to get bored with her, you have to give her things. Look here!"

He went back to the car and opened the trunk. "In the first place," he said, "she needs plenty of clothes—like this gorgeous evening gown, for instance."

He pulled out a gown and tossed it to Momo.

"And here's a genuine mink coat, and a tennis dress, and a skiing outfit, and a swimsuit, and a riding habit, and some pajamas, and a nightie, and another dress, and another, and another, and another . . ."

One by one, he tossed them over till they formed a whole heap on the ground between Momo and the doll.

"There," he said with another thin-lipped smile, "that should keep you happy for a while, shouldn't it? Or are you going to get bored again after a couple of days? Very well, you'll just have to have some more nice things for your doll."

And he reached inside the trunk again.

"Here, for instance, is a real little snakeskin purse with a real little lipstick and powder compact inside. Here's a miniature camera, and a tennis racket, and a doll's TV set that really works. Here's a bracelet, a necklace, some earrings, a doll's gold-plated automatic, some silk stockings, a feather boa, a straw hat, an Easter bonnet, some miniature golf clubs, a little checkbook, perfume, bath salts, body lotion . . ." He broke off and glanced keenly at Momo, who was sitting amid this clutter of toys with a stunned expression on her face.

"You see," he said, "it's quite simple. As long as you go on getting more and more things, you'll never grow bored. I know what you're going to say: Sooner or later, Lola will have *everything*, and then I'll be bored again. Well, there's no fear of that. Here we have the perfect boyfriend for Lola."

This time, when he reached into the trunk, he produced a boy doll. It was the same size as Lola and just as lifelike. "Look," he said, "this is Butch. He has any number of nice things, too, and when you get bored with him we can supply a girlfriend for Lola with masses of outfits that won't fit anyone but her. Butch has a friend, too, and his friend has friends of his own, and so on ad infinitum. So you see, you need never get bored because the game can go on forever. There's always something left to wish for."

As he spoke, the man in gray took doll after doll from the trunk, whose contents seemed inexhaustible. Momo continued to sit there, watching him rather apprehensively, while he arrayed them on the ground beside her.

"Well," he said at length, expelling a dense cloud of smoke from his cigar, "now do you see how to play with dolls like these?"

"Yes," said Momo, who was positively shaking with cold.

Satisfied, the man in gray nodded and took another pull at his cigar. "You'd like to keep all these nice things, wouldn't you? Of course you would. Very well, I'll make you a present of them. You can have them—not all at once, of course, but one at a time—and lots of other things as well. You don't have to do anything in return, just play with them the way I've shown you. What do you say?"

He fixed Momo with an expectant smile. Then, when she still said nothing, just returned his gaze without smiling back, he went on quickly, "You won't need your friends anymore, don't you see? You'll have quite enough to amuse you when all these lovely things are yours and you keep on getting more, won't you? You'd like that, wouldn't you? Surely you want this marvelous doll? I'll bet you've already set your heart on it!"

Momo dimly sensed that she had a fight on her hands—

indeed, that she was already in the thick of the fray—but she didn't know why she was fighting or with whom. The longer she listened to this stranger, the more she felt as she had felt with the doll: she could hear a voice speaking and hear the words it uttered, but she couldn't tell who was actually saying them. She shook her head.

"What!" exclaimed the man in gray, raising his eyebrows. "You modern children are never satisfied, honestly! Lola's perfect in every detail. If there's anything wrong with her, perhaps you'd care to tell me."

Momo stared at the ground and thought hard. Then she said, very quietly, "I don't think anyone could love it—her, I mean."

The man in gray didn't answer for some time. He stared into space with eyes as glassy as the doll's. At last he pulled himself together. "That's not the point," he said coldly.

Momo met his eye. What scared her most about him was the icy chill that seemed to emanate from his body, yet in some strange way—she couldn't have said why—she felt sorry for him as well as scared.

"But I do love my friends," she said.

The man in gray grimaced as if he'd bitten into a lemon, but he quickly recovered his composure and gave her a razor-sharp smile. "Momo," he said smoothly, "I think we should have a serious talk, you and I. It's time you learned what matters in life." He produced a little gray notebook from his pocket and leafed through it until he found what he was looking for. "Your name *is* Momo, isn't it?"

Momo nodded. The man in gray shut his notebook with a snap and pocketed it again. Then, with a faint grunt of exertion, he sat himself down on the ground at Momo's side. He said no more for a while, just puffed thoughtfully at his small gray cigar.

"All right, Momo," he said at last, "listen carefully."

Momo had been trying to do this all the time, but the man in gray was far harder to listen to than anyone she'd ever heard. She could understand what other people meant and what they were like by getting right inside them, so to speak, but with him this was quite impossible. Whenever she tried to read his thoughts she seemed to plunge headlong into a dark chasm, as if there were nothing there at all. It had never happened to her before.

"All that matters in life," the man in gray went on, "is to climb the ladder of success, amount to something, own things. When a person climbs higher than the rest, amounts to more, owns more things, everything else comes automatically: friendship, love, respect, *et cetera.* You tell me you love your friends. Let's examine that statement quite objectively."

He blew a few smoke rings. Momo tucked her bare feet under her skirt and burrowed still deeper into her oversize jacket.

"The first question to consider," pursued the man in gray, "is how much your friends really gain from the fact of your existence. Are you any practical use to them? No. Do you help them to get on in the world, make more money, make something of their lives? No again. Do you assist them in their efforts to save time? On the contrary, you distract them—you're a millstone around their necks and an obstacle to their progress. You may not realize it, Momo, but you harm your friends by simply being here. Without meaning to be, you're really their enemy. Is that what you call love?"

Momo didn't know what to say. She'd never looked at things that way. She even wondered, for one brief moment, whether the man in gray might not be right after all.

"And that," he went on, "is why we want to protect your friends from you. If you really love them, you'll help us. We have their interests at heart, so we want them to succeed in life. We can't just look on idly while you distract them from everything that matters. We want to make sure you leave them alone—that's why we're giving you all these lovely things."

Momo's lips had begun to tremble. "Who's 'we'?" she asked.

"The Timesaving Bank," said the man in gray. "I'm Agent No. BLW/553/c. I wish you no harm, personally speaking, but the Timesaving Bank isn't an organization to be trifled with."

Just then, Momo recalled what Beppo and Guido had said about timesaving being infectious, and she had an awful suspicion that this stranger had something to do with the spread of the epidemic. She wished from the bottom of her heart that her friends were with her now. She had never felt so alone, but she was determined not to let fear get the better of her. Summoning up all her courage, she plunged headlong into the dark chasm in which the stranger concealed his true self.

He had been watching her out of the corner of his eye, so the change in her expression did not escape him. He lit a fresh cigar from the butt of the old one.

"Don't bother," he said with a sarcastic smile. "You're no match for us."

But Momo stood firm. "Isn't there anyone who loves *you?*" she whispered.

The man in gray squirmed a little. "I must say," he replied in his grayest voice, "I've never met anyone like you before, truly I haven't, and I've met a lot of people in my time. If there were many more like you around, we'd have nothing left to live on. We'd have to close down the Timesaving Bank and dissolve into thin air."

He broke off, staring at Momo as if she were something he could neither understand nor cope with. His face turned a shade grayer. When next he spoke, it was as if he were doing so against his will—as if the words were pouring forth despite him. At the same time, his face became more and more convulsed with horror at what was happening to him. At long last, Momo heard his real voice, which seemed to come from infinitely far away.

"We have to remain unrecognized," he blurted out. "No one must know of our existence or activities. We make sure no one ever remembers us, because we can only carry on our business if we pass unnoticed. It's a wearisome business, too, bleeding people of their time by the hour, minute, and second. All the time they save, they lose to us. We drain it off, we hoard it, we thirst for it. Human beings have no conception of the value of their time, but *we* do. We suck them dry, and we need more and more time every day, because there are more and more of us. More and more and more . . ."

The last few words were uttered in a sort of death rattle. The man in gray clapped his hands over his mouth and stared at Momo with his eyes bulging. Little by little, he seemed to emerge from a kind of trance.

"W-what happened?" he stammered. "You've been spying on me! I'm ill, and it's all your fault!" His tone became almost imploring. "I've been talking nonsense, Momo. Forget it— forget me like everyone else. You must, you *must!*"

He grabbed hold of Momo and shook her. Her lips moved, but she couldn't get a word out.

The man in gray jumped to his feet. He peered in all directions like a cornered beast, then snatched up his briefcase and sprinted to the car. The next moment, something very strange happened. Like an explosion in reverse, all the dolls and their scattered belongings flew back into the trunk, which slammed shut. The car roared off at such a speed that grit and pebbles spurted from its wheels.

Momo sat there for a long time, trying to make sense of what she had heard. As the dreadful chill seeped slowly from

her limbs, so her thoughts became steadily clearer. Now that she had heard the real voice of the man in gray, she could remember everything.

From the sunbaked grass in front of her rose a slender thread of smoke. The trampled butt of a small gray cigar was smoldering away to ashes.

EIGHT

The Demonstration

LATE THAT AFTERNOON, Guido and Beppo turned up. They found Momo sitting in the shade of a wall, still rather pale and upset, so they sat down beside her and anxiously inquired what the matter was. Momo began to tell them what had happened, haltingly at first, but she ended by repeating her entire conversation with the man in gray, word for word.

Old Beppo watched her gravely and intently throughout, the furrows in his wrinkled brow growing deeper by the minute. He said nothing, even when she had finished.

Guido, by contrast, listened to her with mounting excitement. His eyes began to shine as they so often did when he himself was telling a story and got carried away. He gripped Momo by the shoulder.

"Well," he said, "this is our big moment. You've discovered something no one else knew. Now we can rescue everyone from their clutches—not just our friends but the whole city! It's up to the three of us—you, me, and Beppo!"

He jumped up and stood there with his arms outflung. In

his mind's eye he could see a vast crowd of people hailing him as their savior.

"Yes," said Momo, looking rather baffled, "but how?"

"What do you mean, 'how'?" Guido demanded irritably.

"I mean," said Momo, "how do we beat the men in gray at their own game?"

Guido shrugged. "I can't say exactly, of course, not right this minute. We'll have to work something out first, but one thing's for sure: now we know they exist and what they're up to, we must tackle them—or are you scared?"

Momo nodded uneasily. "I don't think they're ordinary men. The one that was here looked different, somehow, and the air around him was dreadfully cold. If there are a lot of them, they're bound to be dangerous. Yes, I'm scared all right."

"Don't be silly," Guido said briskly. "The whole thing's quite simple. They can only do their dirty work as long as nobody recognizes them—your visitor said so himself. Well, then! All we have to do is make sure they're recognizable. Once people recognize them they'll remember them, and once they remember them they'll know them again at a glance. The men in gray won't be able to harm us then—we'll be safe as houses."

"You really think so?" Momo said rather doubtfully.

Guido's eyes were alight with confidence. "Of course," he assured her. "Why else would your visitor have taken to his heels like that? They're terrified of us, I tell you."

"What if we can't find them?" Momo asked. "They may go and hide."

"They may well," Guido conceded. "If they do, we'll simply have to lure them out into the open."

"But how?" asked Momo. "They're pretty smart, it seems to me."

"That's easy," Guido said with a chuckle. "We'll take advantage of their own greed. If you can catch mice with cheese, you can catch time-thieves with time—and that we've got plenty of. For instance, Beppo and I could lie in wait while you sat here twiddling your thumbs. When they took the bait, we'd jump out and overpower them."

"But they know me already," Momo objected. "I don't think they'd fall for it."

"All right," said Guido, who was brimming over with bright ideas, "then we'll try something else. Your man in gray mentioned something about a Timesaving Bank. That means it's a building somewhere in town. All we have to do is find it, and find it we will, because it's bound to be a very special-looking place. I can see it now—gray, sinister, and windowless, like a gigantic concrete safe. Once we find it, we'll walk straight in. We'll all be armed with pistols, one in each hand. 'You!' I'll say. 'Hand over the time you've stolen, and make it snappy!' And they'll—"

"But we don't have any pistols," Momo broke in anxiously.

Guido grandly dismissed this objection. "Then we'll do it unarmed. That'll impress them even more. They'll panic at the very sight of us."

"It might be better if there were a few more of us," Momo said. "I mean, we'd probably find the Timesaving Bank quicker if other people went looking for it too."

"Good idea," said Guido. "We must mobilize all our friends—and all the kids who spend so much time here nowadays. I vote we get started right away, the three of us. Tell as many people as you can find, and tell them to pass the word. We'll all meet up here at three tomorrow afternoon, for a grand council of war."

So they all set off at once, Momo in one direction, Beppo and Guido in another.

The two men had gone some distance when Beppo, who still hadn't spoken, came to a sudden stop. "Know something, Guido?" he said. "I'm worried."

Guido turned to look at him. "About what?"

Beppo regarded his friend in silence for a moment. Then he said, "I believe Momo."

"So do I," said Guido, puzzled. "What of it?"

"I mean," Beppo went on, "I believe that what she told us is true."

Guido couldn't understand what the old man was getting at. "Of course," he said. "So what?"

"Well," said Beppo, "if it's true what she told us, we shouldn't rush into anything. We don't want to tangle with a bunch of crooks just like that, do we? If we provoke them, it may land Momo in trouble. I don't mind so much about us, but we may endanger the children if we bring them into it too. We must think very carefully before we act."

Guido threw back his head and laughed. "You and your eternal worrying!" he scoffed. "The more of us there are, the better. That's obvious."

"From the sound of it," Beppo said gravely, "you don't believe that Momo's story was true at all."

"Depends what you mean by 'true,'" Guido retorted. "You've no imagination, that's your trouble. The whole world's one big story and we're all part of it. Sure I believe what Momo told us, Beppo—every word of it, just like you."

Beppo could find no suitable response to this, but Guido's optimism did nothing to allay his fears.

Then they parted company, Guido with a light heart, Beppo filled with foreboding, and went off to spread the news of tomorrow's meeting.

That night Guido dreamed he was being feted as one of the city's saviors. He saw himself in a dress suit, Beppo in a smart cutaway, and Momo in a snow-white silk gown. The mayor draped gold chains around their necks and crowned them with laurel wreaths. Stirring music rang out, and the citizens honored their deliverers with a torchlight procession longer and more impressive than any that had ever been seen before.

Meanwhile, old Beppo was tossing and turning, unable to sleep. The more he thought about what lay ahead, the more clearly he perceived its dangers. He wouldn't let Guido and Momo brave them alone. He would stand by them whatever happened—that went without saying—but he must at least attempt to dissuade them.

By three the next afternoon, the amphitheater resounded to excited cries and the hum of many voices. Although it saddened Momo that none of her grown-up friends had appeared —except, of course, for Beppo and Guido—some fifty or sixty children had come from near and far. They were all shapes and sizes, rich and poor, well-behaved and rowdy. Some, like Maria, were holding younger members of the family by the hand or in their arms—tiny little children who sucked their thumbs and gazed wide-eyed at this unusual gathering.

Franco, Paolo, and Massimo were there too, naturally, but most of the other children were relative newcomers to the amphitheater, and they had a special interest in the subject under discussion. Among them was the owner of the transistor radio, who had turned up without it. Seating himself next to Momo, he told her straight away that his name was Claudio, and that he was glad to have been invited.

When it became clear that the last of the children had arrived, Guido rose to his feet and, with a sweeping gesture, called for silence. The buzz of conversation died away, and an expectant hush descended on the amphitheater.

"My friends," Guido began, "you all have a rough idea why we're here—you were told when you received your invitations to this secret meeting. More and more people are finding themselves with less and less time to spare, even though they're saving it for all they're worth. The truth is, they've lost the very time they meant to save. Why? We now know, thanks to Momo. People are being robbed of their time—and I mean robbed—by a gang of time-thieves! That's why we need your help: so as to put a stop to the activities of this cold-blooded, criminal fraternity. Our city is in the grip of a nightmare. With your cooperation, we can banish it at a stroke. Isn't that a cause worth fighting for?"

He paused while the children applauded.

"We'll discuss what to do in due course," he went on. "Meantime, Momo is going to describe her encounter with a member of the gang and how he gave himself away."

"One moment," said Beppo, getting up. "Listen, children!
I say Momo *shouldn't* tell you her story. It's a bad idea. If she
does, she'll endanger herself and all of you."

"No," cried several voices, "let her speak! We want
Momo!" More and more voices joined in until all the children
were chanting "Momo, Momo, Momo!" in unison.

Old Beppo sat down again. He took off his little steel-
rimmed spectacles and wearily rubbed his eyes.

Momo stood up, looking perplexed. She didn't know whose
wishes to comply with, Beppo's or the children's. At length,
while her audience listened attentively, she recounted what
had happened.

A long silence fell when she was finished. The children had
grown rather uneasy during her recital. They hadn't imagined
that time-thieves could be so sinister. One tiny tot burst into
tears but was quickly comforted.

The silence was broken by Guido. "Well," he said, "how
many of you have the guts to join our campaign against the
men in gray?"

"Why didn't Beppo want Momo to tell us what happened?"
Franco inquired.

Guido gave him a reassuring smile. "He thinks the time-
thieves feel threatened by those who know their secret, so
they try to hunt them down. Myself, I think it's the other way
around. I'm convinced that knowing their secret makes a person invulnerable: once you know it they can't lay a finger on
you. That's logical, wouldn't you say? Come on, Beppo, admit
it!"

But Beppo only shook his head, and the children remained
silent.

"One thing's certain, anyway," Guido pursued. "From now
on we must stick together come hell or high water. We've got
to be careful, but we mustn't get scared. All right, I'll ask you
again: Who's prepared to join us?"

"I am!" said Claudio, getting to his feet. He looked a trifle
pale.

Others followed suit, hesitantly at first, then more and more resolutely, until everyone present had volunteered.

"Well, Beppo," said Guido, pointing to the forest of raised hands, "what do you say now?"

Beppo nodded sadly. "I'm with you too, of course."

"Good." Guido turned back to the children. "So now let's decide what to do. Any suggestions?"

They all thought hard. Paolo, the boy with glasses, finally said, "But how do they do it? I mean, can they really steal time?"

"Yes," Claudio chimed in. "What *is* time, anyway?"

No one could supply an answer.

Maria, with little Rosa in her arms, got up from her seat on the far side of the arena. "Maybe it's like electricity," she hazarded. "After all, there are machines that can record people's thought waves—I've seen one myself, on TV. They've got gadgets that can do anything these days."

"How about this for an idea!" squeaked Massimo, the fat boy with the high-pitched voice. "When you photograph something, it's down on film. When you record something, it's down on tape. Maybe they've got a machine that can record time. If we knew where it was, we could simply put it into reverse and the missing time would be there again!"

"Anyway," said Paolo, adjusting his glasses, "the first thing to do is find a scientist to help us. We won't get anywhere without one."

"You and your scientists!" sneered Franco. "Who says *they* can be trusted? Suppose we found one who was an expert on time. How could we be sure he wasn't in league with the time-thieves? Then we'd really be up the creek!"

Everyone seemed impressed by this objection.

The next person to speak up was a little girl of demure and ladylike appearance. "If you ask me," she said, "our best plan would be to go to the police and tell them the whole story."

"Now I've heard everything!" Franco scoffed. "What could the cops do? These aren't just ordinary thieves. Either the cops have known about them all along, in which case they must be powerless, or they haven't noticed a thing, in which case they'd never believe us."

A baffled silence ensued.

"Well," Paolo said eventually, "we've got to do *something*— as soon as possible, too, before the time-thieves get wind of what we're up to."

Guido rose to his feet again.

"My friends," he said, "I've already given this matter a lot of thought. After dreaming up hundreds of schemes and rejecting them all in turn, I finally hit on one that's guaranteed to do the trick—as long as you all cooperate. I merely wanted to see if one of you could come up with a better idea. Well, now I'll tell you what we're going to do."

He paused and looked slowly around the amphitheater. He was ringed by fifty or sixty expectant faces, the biggest audience he'd had in a long time.

"As you're now aware," he went on, "the men in gray depend for their power on being able to work unrecognized and in secret. It follows that the simplest and most effective way of rendering them harmless is to broadcast the truth about them. And how are we to do that? I'll tell you. We're going to hold a mass demonstration! We're going to paint posters and banners and march through the streets with them. We're going to attract as much attention as possible. We're going to invite *the whole city* to join us here, at the old amphitheater, to hear the full facts."

A stir ran through the listening children.

"Everyone will go wild with excitement," Guido continued. "Thousands and thousands of people will come flocking in. Then, when a vast crowd has assembled, we'll reveal the whole terrible truth. And then, my friends, the world will change overnight. No one will be able to steal people's time anymore. They'll all have as much as they need, because there'll be enough to go around again. That's what we can achieve if we all work together—if we're all in favor. Are we?"

This drew a chorus of exultant yells.

"Carried unanimously," said Guido. "In that case, we'll

invite the whole city here next Sunday afternoon. Till then, though, we mustn't breathe a word of our plan. And now, let's get to work.''

For the next few days, the amphitheater hummed with furtive but feverish activity. Sheets of paper, pots of paint, brushes, paste, cardboard, poles, planks, and a host of other

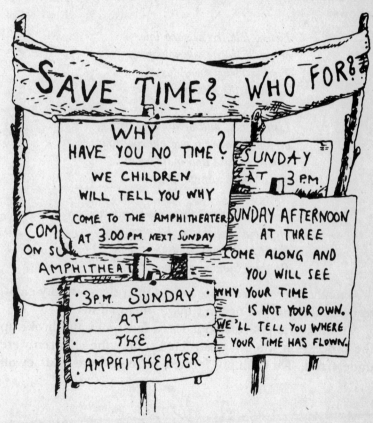

essentials appeared like magic—where from, the children preferred not to say. Some of them made banners and posters and placards, while others—the ones that were good at writing—thought up catchy slogans and painted them in their neatest lettering.

At last, when all was ready, the children assembled in the amphitheater and set off in single file with Guido, Beppo, and Momo at their head. They marched through the streets brandishing posters and banners, clattering saucepan lids, blowing penny whistles, chanting slogans, and singing a song composed specially for the occasion by Guido. The words went as follows:

> *Listen, folk, ere it's too late,*
> *or you'll live to rue your fate.*
> *Time is flying every day,*
> *stolen by the men in gray.*

> *Listen, folk, and heed our warning,*
> *or you'll wake up one fine morning*
> *robbed of time and quite bereft,*
> *not a single minute left.*

> *Don't save time, then, save your city,*
> *for those time-thieves have no pity.*
> *Fight back hard, and do it soon.*
> *Be there Sunday afternoon!*

Actually, there were more verses than that—twenty-eight, to be exact—but we needn't quote them all here.

Although the police stepped in a few times and broke up the procession when it obstructed traffic, the children were undeterred. They simply formed up elsewhere and set off

again. Nothing happened apart from this, and they didn't sight a single man in gray for all their vigilance.

They were, however, joined by other children who saw the demonstration and hadn't known of the affair till now. More and more youngsters tagged along until the streets were filled with hundreds or even thousands of them, all urging their elders to attend the meeting that was to change the world.

NINE

The Trial

THE GREAT MOMENT had come and gone.

It was over, and not a single grown-up had appeared. The children's demonstration had passed almost unnoticed by the very people it was aimed at. All their efforts had been in vain.

The big red sun was already sinking into a sea of purple cloud, so low in the sky that its rays lit only the topmost tier of steps in the amphitheater, where so many hundreds of children had been waiting for so long. No cheerful hum of voices broke the sad and disconsolate silence.

The shadows were lengthening fast. It would soon be dark, and the children began to shiver in the chill evening air. Somewhere in the distance a church clock struck eight. Doubt gave way to certainty: the whole scheme had been a complete fiasco.

One or two children got up and drifted off. Others followed suit. None of them said a word—their disappointment was too great.

Eventually, Paolo came over to Momo and said, "It's no use

waiting any longer—no one'll turn up now. Good night." And he walked off too.

Franco was the next to leave. "It's hopeless," he said. "We can't count on the grown-ups, we know that now. I never did trust them anyway. As far as I'm concerned, they can stew in their own juice from now on."

More and more children left. It was dark by the time the last of them gave up and went home, leaving Momo alone with Guido and Beppo.

The old roadsweeper stood up.

"Are you going too?" Momo asked.

"I've got to," Beppo told her with a sigh. "I'm on night duty."

"*Night* duty?"

"Yes, unloading garbage at the municipal dump. I'm due there in half an hour."

"But it's Sunday. Besides, you've never had to do that before."

"No, but we've been told to report there. They say it's only temporary. There's too much garbage to handle, apparently. Shortage of staff, and so on."

"What a shame," said Momo. "I'd have liked you to stay awhile."

"Yes, I don't want to go myself, but there it is—I've got to." And Beppo mounted his squeaky old bicycle and pedaled off into the darkness.

Guido was whistling a soft and melancholy tune. He could whistle very sweetly, and Momo was listening with pleasure when he suddenly broke off.

"Heavens," he exclaimed, "I must go too. Today's when I start my new job—night watchman, didn't I tell you? I'd forgotten the time."

Momo just stared at him and said nothing.

"So our plan didn't work out," he went on. "Never mind, Momo. It didn't work out the way I hoped, either, but it was fun all the same—tremendous fun."

When Momo still said nothing, he stroked her hair soothingly and added, "Don't take it so hard, Momo. Everything'll look quite different in the morning. We'll just have to come up with a new idea—a new game, eh?"

"It wasn't a game," Momo said in a muffled voice.

Guido stood up. "Look, I know how you feel, but we'll talk about it tomorrow, okay? I have to go now—I'm late enough as it is. Anyway, it's time you went to bed."

And he walked off whistling his melancholy tune.

So Momo remained sitting forlornly in the great stone bowl of the amphitheater. Clouds had veiled the sky and blotted out the stars. A peculiar breeze had sprung up, light but persistent and singularly cold. If breezes can be said to have a color, this one was gray.

Far away beyond the outskirts of the city loomed the massive municipal garbage dump. It was a veritable mountain of ash, cinders, broken glass and china, tin cans, plastic containers, old mattresses, cardboard cartons, and countless other objects discarded by the city's inhabitants, all waiting to be fed, bit by bit, into huge incinerators.

Beppo and his fellow workers toiled for hours, shoveling garbage out of a long line of trucks. The trucks crept forward, headlights blazing, but the more they emptied the longer the line became.

"Faster!" the foreman kept shouting. "Hurry it up, or we'll never be through!"

They didn't finish the job till midnight, by which time Beppo's shirt was clinging to his back. Being older than the rest and not the most robust of men, he flopped down wearily on an upturned plastic bucket and struggled to get his breath back.

"Hey, Beppo," one of his fellow workers called, "we're going home now. Coming?"

"In a minute," wheezed Beppo. He clasped one hand to his aching chest.

"Feeling all right, old man?" called someone else.

"I'm fine," Beppo called back. "Just taking a little breather, that's all. Don't wait for me."

"Okay," said the others, "good night." And off they went. It was quiet when they'd gone, except for an occasional rustle and squeak from rats scrabbling in the garbage. Beppo pillowed his head on his folded arms and dozed off.

He didn't know how long he'd been asleep when he was roused by a gust of cold air. One look was enough to jolt him awake in an instant.

All over the huge mound of garbage stood gray figures attired in smart gray suits and gray derbies, steel gray brief-cases in their hands and small gray cigars in their mouths. They were gazing fixedly, silently, at the summit of the mound. There, ensconced on a sort of magistrates' bench, sat three men identical to the others in every respect.

Beppo was frightened for a moment. He had no business being there—he sensed that instinctively—and the prospect of discovery scared him. Very soon, however, he realized that the army of gray figures had eyes for no one but the three-man tribunal. Either they had failed to notice him at all, or they had mistaken him for some discarded object. Whatever the explanation, he resolved to keep as still as a mouse.

Then the silence was broken by a voice from the judges' bench. "The Supreme Court is now in session," announced the central figure. "Call Agent No. BLW/553/c."

The cry was repeated farther down the slope and repeated again some distance away, like an echo. Threading his way slowly through the crowd and up the mound of garbage came a man in gray, distinguishable from his fellows only by the pallor of his face, which was almost white.

At last he reached the tribunal.

"You are Agent No. BLW/553/c?" asked the man in the center.

"I am."

"How long have you been employed by the Timesaving Bank?"

"Ever since I came into existence, Your Honor."

"That goes without saying—kindly spare us such irrelevancies. When did you come into existence?"

"Eleven years, three months, six days, eight hours, thirty-two minutes, and—at this precise moment—eighteen seconds ago."

Oddly enough, although this exchange was being conducted a long way off and in low, monotonous voices, Beppo didn't miss a word of it.

"Are you aware," the man in the center went on, "that a substantial number of children paraded through the streets today with placards and banners, and that they even entertained the outrageous notion of inviting the whole city to attend a briefing on our activities?"

"It hadn't escaped me," replied the agent.

"How do you account for the fact that these children knew about us and our activities?" the senior inquisitor pursued remorselessly.

"It's a mystery to me, your honor," said the agent. "If I may venture a personal observation, however, I would urge the Supreme Court not to take this incident more seriously than it deserves. It was a piece of childish nonsense, that's all. I would also urge the court to bear in mind that we easily managed to scotch the scheduled meeting by leaving people no time to attend it. Even had we failed to do so, however, I'm confident that everyone would have dismissed the children's information as a cock-and-bull story. In my opinion, we would have done better to let the meeting go ahead, because that would—"

"Defendant!" the judge broke in sharply. "Do you realize where you are?"

The agent wilted. "Yes," he whispered.

"This is no human court," the judge continued. "You are being tried by your own kind. Lying to us is futile, you know that perfectly well, so why bother to try?"

"It's—it's an occupational habit," the agent stammered.

"It is for this court to decide how seriously to take the children's intentions. However, I need hardly remind you that children present a greater threat to our work than anyone or anything else."

"I know," the agent conceded meekly.

"Children," declared the judge, "are our natural enemies. But for them, mankind would have been completely in our power long ago. Adults are far easier to turn into timesavers. That's why one of our most sacred commandments states, 'Leave the children till last.' Are you familiar with that commandment, defendant?"

"Yes indeed, your honor," said the agent, puffing hard at his cigar. It was a peculiar fact that, despite the solemnity of the occasion, all present—judges, defendant, and spectators —were smoking incessantly.

"And yet," the judge retorted, "we have incontrovertible proof that one of us—I repeat, *one of us*—not only got into a conversation with a child but betrayed us. Do you happen to know who that certain person was?"

Agent No. BLW/553/c wilted still more. "It was me, your honor."

"And why did you break our most sacred commandment?"

"Because the child in question has been seriously impeding our work by turning people against us. I had the interests of the Timesaving Bank at heart. My intentions were of the best."

"Your intentions don't concern us," the judge said icily. "Results are all that count here, and the result of your unauthorized action has been to gain us no time and acquaint a child with some of our most vital secrets. Do you admit that?"

The agent hung his head. "I do," he whispered.

"So you plead guilty?"

"Yes, your honor, but I would draw the court's attention to an extenuating circumstance: I was genuinely bewitched— lured into betraying us by the way the child listened to me. I can't explain how it happened, but I swear that's the way it was."

"Your excuses are irrelevant and immaterial. This court takes no account of extenuating circumstances. The law is quite categorical on this point and allows of no exceptions. However, we shall certainly devote some attention to this unusual child. What is its name?"

"Momo, your honor."

"Male or female?"

"She's a girl."

"Place of residence?"

"The ruined amphitheater."

"Very well," said the judge, who had recorded all these details in his notebook. "You may rest assured, defendant, that this child will never harm us again—we shall neutralize her by every available means. Let that thought console you, now that sentence is about to be passed and carried out."

The agent began to tremble. "What is the sentence?" he whispered.

The three judges put their heads together and conferred in an undertone. Then they nodded, and their spokesman turned to face the prisoner again.

"Agent No. BLW/553/c having pleaded guilty to a charge of high treason, this court unanimously sentences him to pay the penalty prescribed by law. He is to be deprived of all time forthwith."

"Mercy, mercy!" shrieked the agent, but his steel gray briefcase and small cigar had already been snatched away by two gray figures standing beside him.

And then a very strange thing happened. No sooner had the condemned man lost his cigar than he started to become more and more transparent. His screams grew fainter, too, as he stood there with his head in his hands, dissolving into thin air. The last that could be seen of him was a little flurry of ash eddying in the breeze, but that soon vanished too.

Silently the men in gray dispersed, judges and spectators alike. Once the darkness had swallowed them up, the sole reminder of their presence was a chill, gray wind that swirled around the dismal and deserted garbage dump.

Beppo continued to sit spellbound on his upturned bucket, staring at the spot where the condemned man had been standing. He felt as if his limbs had turned to ice and were only just beginning to thaw. The men in gray existed; he had seen them for himself.

At about the same time—the distant church clock had already struck twelve—Momo was still sitting on the steps of the amphitheater. She was waiting. For what, she didn't know, but some instinct had dissuaded her from going to bed.

All of a sudden, something lightly brushed against her bare foot. Peering hard, for it was very dark, she saw a big tortoise looking up at her. Its mouth seemed to curve in a mysterious smile, and there was such a friendly light in its shrewd, black eyes that Momo felt it was about to speak.

She bent down and tickled it under the chin. "Who might you be?" she said softly. "Nice of you to come and keep me company, Tortoise, even if nobody else will. What can I do for you?"

Momo wasn't sure whether she'd failed to notice them before, or whether they'd only just appeared, but she suddenly spotted some letters on the tortoise's back. They were faintly

luminous and seemed to follow the natural patterns on its shell.

FOLLOW ME, she slowly deciphered.

Astonished, she sat up with a jerk. "Do you mean me?" she asked.

But the tortoise had already set off. After a few steps it paused and looked back. "It really does mean me!" Momo said to herself. She got up and went over to the creature. "Keep going," she told it softly, "I'm right behind you."

And step by step she followed the tortoise as it slowly, very slowly, led her out of the amphitheater and headed for the city.

TEN

More Haste Less Speed

OLD BEPPO was pedaling through the darkness on his squeaky bicycle—pedaling with all his might. The gray judge's words still rang in his ears: "We shall certainly devote some attention to this unusual child . . . You may rest assured that this child will never harm us again . . . We shall neutralize her by every available means . . ."

Momo was in dire peril, of that there could be no doubt. He must go to her at once, warn her and protect her from the men in gray. He didn't know how, but he'd find a way. Beppo pedaled even faster, his tuft of white hair fluttering in the breeze. He still had a long way to go.

The ruined amphitheater was ablaze with the headlights of a whole fleet of smart gray cars, which hemmed it in on every side. Dozens of men in gray were scurrying up and down the grass-grown steps. At last, after peering into every nook and cranny, they came upon the hole in the wall. Some of them scrambled through it into Momo's room. They looked under the bed—they even looked inside the little brick stove. Then they reappeared, patted the dust from their smart gray suits, and shrugged.

"The bird appears to have flown," said one.

"It's exasperating," said another. "Children should be safely tucked in bed at this hour, not gallivanting around in the dark."

"I don't like the look of this," said a third. "It's almost as if someone had tipped her off just in time."

"Impossible," said the first. "He couldn't have known of our intention before we knew it ourselves—or could he?"

The three of them eyed each other in dismay.

"If someone really did tip her off," the third pointed out, "she'll have made herself scarce. We'll only be wasting time if we go on looking for her here."

"What do you suggest, then?"

"I say we should notify headquarters at once, so they can launch a full-scale manhunt."

"The first thing they'll ask us—and quite rightly so—is whether we've made a thorough search of the immediate neighborhood."

"Very well," said the first speaker, "let's search the area first, but if the girl's well clear of it already, we'll be making a big mistake."

"Nonsense," snapped his colleague. "Even if she is, headquarters can still launch a full-scale manhunt using every available agent. The girl won't escape—she doesn't stand a chance. Right, gentlemen, let's get going. You all know what's at stake."

Many of the local inhabitants lay awake that night, wondering why so many cars kept racing past their windows. Even the narrowest side streets and roughest farm tracks resounded until daybreak with a roar of traffic more usually heard on major highways. No one could sleep a wink.

All this time, Momo was trudging slowly through the city in the wake of her newfound friend, the tortoise. The city never slept nowadays, however late the hour. Interminable streams of people surged through the streets, jostling and elbowing each other aside. The roadways were choked with cars and big, noisy, overcrowded buses. Neon signs blazed down from every building, intermittently bathing passers-by in their multicolored glare.

Momo, who had never seen any of this before, followed the tortoise in a kind of wide-eyed, waking dream. They made their way across broad squares and down brightly lit streets. Cars flashed past them and pedestrians milled around them, but no one looked twice at the child and the tortoise.

They never had to get out of anyone's way, either. Nobody bumped into them, nor did any driver have to brake to avoid them. The tortoise seemed to know precisely when there would be no car or pedestrian in their path, so they never had to vary their pace, never had to hurry or to stop and wait. Momo began to wonder how any two creatures could walk so slowly but travel so fast.

When Beppo finally reached the amphitheater, the feeble glow of his bicycle lamp showed him, even before he dismounted, that the ground around it was a mass of tire tracks. He left his bicycle in the grass and ran to the hole in the wall.

"Momo!" He whispered the name at first, then spoke it aloud. "Momo!" he repeated.

No answer.

Beppo swallowed hard, his throat felt so dry. He climbed through the hole into the pitch-black room, stumbled over something, and wrenched his ankle. Striking a match with tremulous fingers, he peered in all directions.

The crude little table and chairs were overturned, the blankets and mattress stripped off the bed. Of Momo herself, there was no sign at all.

Beppo bit his lip to stifle the hoarse sob that racked his chest at the sight of this desolation. "My God," he muttered, "I'm too late. She's gone—they've spirited the poor girl away. What shall I do now? What *can* I do?" Just then the match

began to burn his fingers, so he dropped it and stood there in the dark.

Making his way outside as fast as his twisted ankle would allow, he hobbled over to his bicycle, struggled back into the saddle, and pedaled off again. "Guido must help," he kept repeating, "—he must! Pray heaven I can find him!"

He knew that Guido planned to earn some extra money by spending Sunday nights in the storeroom of a car wrecker's junkyard. Serviceable parts had been disappearing of late, and it was Guido's job to see that this pilfering ceased.

When Beppo ran him to ground in a shed beside the junkyard and hammered on the door with his fist, Guido at first mistook him for a would-be stealer of spare parts and kept mum. Then, recognizing the old man's voice, he unlocked the door.

"What's the matter?" he grumbled.

"It's Momo," Beppo told him breathlessly. "She's in danger."

"What are you talking about?" asked Guido, flopping down on his camp bed. "Momo? Why, what's happened to her?"

"I don't know, exactly," Beppo panted, "but it doesn't look good."

And he told Guido all he'd seen, from the trial on the garbage dump, to the tire tracks around the amphitheater, to Momo's ransacked and deserted room. He took quite a while to get it all out, of course, because not even the concern and anxiety he felt for Momo could make him speak any faster than he usually did.

"I knew it all along," he concluded. "I knew it would end in disaster. Well, now they've taken their revenge—they've kid-napped her. We've got to help her, Guido, but how? *How?*"

The blood had slowly drained from Guido's cheeks while Beppo was speaking. He felt as if the ground had given way beneath him. Till now, he'd regarded the whole affair as a splendid game and taken it neither more nor less seriously than he took any game or story. Now, for the first time ever, a story had escaped his control. It had taken on a life of its own, and all the imagination in the world would be insufficient to halt it. He felt numb.

"You know, Beppo," he said after a while, "Momo may simply have gone for a walk. She does that occasionally—like the time she went roaming around the countryside for three whole days and nights. We may be worrying for no good reason."

"What about the tire tracks?" Beppo demanded angrily. "What about the state of her room?"

Guido refused to be drawn. "Suppose they really did come looking for her," he said. "Who's to say they found her? Perhaps she'd gone by the time they got there. Why else would they have searched the place and turned it upside down?"

"But what if they did find her?" Beppo shouted. "What then?" He gripped his young friend by the lapels and shook him. "Don't be a fool, Guido. The men in gray are *real,* I tell you. We've got to do something and fast!"

"Easy," Guido said soothingly, startled by the old man's vehemence. "Of course we'll do something, but not before we've thought it over carefully. After all, we don't even know where to look for her."

Beppo released him. "I'm going to the police," he announced.

"You can't do that!" Guido protested with a look of horror.

"Have some sense, Beppo. Suppose they found her. Don't you know what they'd do with her—don't you know where waifs and strays end up? They'd stick her in a home with bars over the windows. You wouldn't want that, would you?"

"No," Beppo muttered helplessly, "of course not. But what if she's really in trouble?"

"What if she isn't?" Guido argued. "What if she's only gone for a bit of a ramble and you set the police on her. I wouldn't like to be in your shoes then. She might never want to see you again."

Beppo subsided onto a chair and buried his face in his hands. "I just don't know what to do," he groaned, "I just don't know."

"Well," said Guido, "I vote we wait till tomorrow or the day after before we do anything at all. If she still isn't back, okay, we'll go to the police. My guess is, everything will have sorted itself out long before then, and the three of us will be laughing at the whole silly business."

"You think so?" muttered Beppo, suddenly overcome with fatigue. The day's excitements had been a bit too much for a man of his age.

"Of course," Guido assured him. He eased Beppo's boots off and wrapped his sprained ankle in a damp cloth, then helped him onto the camp bed. "Don't worry," he said softly, "everything's going to be fine."

But Beppo was already asleep. Sighing, Guido stretched out on the floor with his jacket under his head in lieu of a pillow. Sleep eluded him, though. He couldn't stop thinking about the men in gray, all night long, and for the first time in his happy-go-lucky life he felt frightened.

The Timesaving Bank had launched a full-scale manhunt. Every agent in the city was instructed by headquarters to drop everything else and concentrate on finding the girl known as Momo.

Every street teemed with gray figures. They lay in wait on rooftops and lurked in sewers, staked out the airport and railroad stations, kept an unobtrusive watch on buses and streetcars—in short, they were everywhere at once.

But they still didn't find the girl known as Momo.

"I say, Tortoise," said Momo, as the pair of them made their way across a darkened courtyard. "Aren't you going to tell me where you're taking me?"

Some letters took shape on the tortoise's shell. DON'T BE SCARED, they read.

"I'm not," said Momo, when she'd deciphered them, though she said it more to boost her courage than anything else. Truth to tell, she did feel rather apprehensive. The tortoise's route was becoming steadily more tortuous and erratic. It had already taken them across parks, over bridges and through subways, into buildings and along corridors—even, once or twice, through cellars.

Had Momo known that she was being hunted by a whole army of men in gray, she would probably have felt uneasier still, but she didn't, so she followed the tortoise patiently, step by step, as it continued to meander along.

It was lucky she did. Just as the creature had previously threaded its way through traffic, so it now seemed to know exactly where and when their pursuers would appear. There were times when the men in gray reached a spot only moments after they themselves had passed it, but hunters and hunted never actually bumped into each other.

"It's a good thing I've learned to read so well," Momo remarked casually, "isn't it?"

Instantly, the tortoise's shell flashed a warning: SSSH!

Momo couldn't understand the reason for this injunction, but she obeyed it. Then she saw three dim, gray shapes flit past a few feet away.

They had now reached a part of the city where each building looked drabber and shabbier than the last. Towering tenements with peeling walls flanked streets pitted with potholes full of stagnant water. The whole neighborhood was dark and deserted.

At long last, word reached the headquarters of the Timesaving Bank that Momo had been sighted.

"Excellent," said the duty officer. "Have you taken her into custody?"

"No, she disappeared before we could nab her—she seemed to vanish from the face of the earth. We've lost track of her again."

"How did it happen?"

"If only we knew! There's something fishy going on."

"Where was she when you sighted her?"

"That's the odd thing. She was in a part of the city completely unknown to us."

"There's no such place," said the duty officer.

"There must be. It seems to be—how shall I put it?—right on the very edge of time, and the girl was heading that way."

"What?" yelped the duty officer. "After her again! You've got to catch her before she gets there—at all costs, is that clear?"

"Understood, sir," came the ashen-voiced answer.

Momo might almost have imagined that day was breaking, except that the strange glow appeared so suddenly—just as they turned a corner, to be exact. It wasn't dark anymore, nor was it light, nor did the glow resemble the half-light of dawn or dusk. It was a radiance that outlined every object with unnatural crispness and clarity, yet it seemed to come from nowhere—or rather, from everywhere at once. The long, black shadows cast by everything, even the tiniest pebble, ran in all directions as if the tree over there were lit from the left, the building over there from the right, the monument over there from dead ahead.

The monument, if that was what it was, looked weird enough in itself. It consisted of a big square block of black stone surmounted by a gigantic white egg, nothing more.

The houses, too, were unlike any Momo had ever seen, with dazzling white walls and windows cloaked in shadows so dark and dense that it was impossible to tell whether anyone lived inside. Somehow, though, Momo sensed that these houses hadn't been built for people to live in, but for some mysterious and quite different purpose.

The streets were completely empty, not only of people but of dogs and cats and birds and cars. Not a movement or breath of wind disturbed the utter stillness. The whole district might have been encased in glass.

Although the tortoise was plodding along more slowly than ever, Momo again found herself marveling at their rate of progress.

Beyond the borders of this strange part of town, where it was still nighttime, three smart gray limousines came racing down the potholed street with headlights blazing. Each was manned by several agents, and one of them, who was in the lead car, caught sight of Momo just as she turned into the street with the white houses and the unearthly glow coming from it.

When they reached the corner, however, something quite incomprehensible happened: the convoy came to a sudden stop. The drivers stepped on the gas. Engines roared and wheels spun, but the cars themselves refused to budge. They might have been on a conveyor belt traveling at exactly the same speed but in the opposite direction, and the more they accelerated the faster it went. By the time the men in gray grasped the truth, Momo was almost out of sight. Cursing, they jumped out and tried to overtake her on foot. They sprinted hard, grimacing with rage and exertion, but much the same thing happened. When they were finally compelled to give up, they had covered a mere ten yards. Meanwhile, Momo had disappeared among the snow-white houses and was nowhere to be seen.

"That's that," said one of the men in gray. "It's no use, we'll never catch her now."

"Why were we rooted to the spot?" demanded another. "I just don't understand it."

"Neither do I," said the first. "The only question is, will

they take that into our favor when we come back empty-handed?"

"You mean they may put us on trial?"

"Well, they certainly won't give us a pat on the back."

All the agents looked downcast. Perching on the fenders and bumpers of their gray limousines, they brooded on the price of failure. There was no point in hurrying, not now.

Far, far away by this time, somewhere in the maze of deserted, snow-white streets and squares, Momo continued to follow the tortoise. Despite their leisurely progress, or because of it, the streets and buildings seemed to flash past in a white blur. The tortoise turned yet another corner, and Momo, following close behind, stopped short in amazement. The street ahead of them was unlike all the rest.

It was really more of an alleyway than a street. The close-packed buildings on either side were a mass of little turrets, oriels, and balconies. They resembled dainty glass palaces which, after lying on the seabed since time out of mind, had suddenly risen to the surface. Draped in seaweed and encrusted with barnacles and coral, they shimmered gently with all the iridescent, rainbow hues of mother-of-pearl.

The narrow street ended in a house detached from all the others and standing at right angles to them. Its big bronze front door was richly decorated with ornamental figures.

Momo glanced up at the street sign immediately above her. It was a slab of white marble, and on it, in gold lettering, were the words NEVER LANE.

Although she had taken only a second or two to look at the sign and read it, the tortoise was already far ahead and had almost reached the house at the end of the lane.

"Wait for me, Tortoise!" she called, but for some strange reason she couldn't hear her own voice.

The tortoise seemed to have heard, though, because it paused and looked around. Momo tried to follow, but no sooner had she set off down Never Lane than a curious sensation gripped her. She felt as if she were toiling upstream against a mighty torrent or battling with an inaudible tempest that threatened to blow her backward. Bent almost double, she braced her body against the mysterious force, hauling herself along hand over hand or crawling on all fours.

She could just make out the little figure of the tortoise waiting patiently at the end of the lane. "I'm getting nowhere!" she called at last. "Help me, can't you?"

Slowly the tortoise retraced its steps. When it came to a halt in front of her, its shell bore the following advice: WALK BACKWARD.

Momo tried it. She turned around and walked backward, and all at once she was progressing up the lane with the utmost ease. At the same time, something most peculiar happened to her. While walking backward, she was also thinking, breathing, and feeling backward—living backward, in fact.

At length she bumped into something solid. Turning, she found she was standing outside the last house of all, the one that stood at right angles to the rest. She gave a little start because, seen at this range, the ornate bronze door looked enormous.

"I wonder if I'll ever get it open," she thought, but at that moment the massive door swung open by itself.

She paused again, distracted by the sight of another sign above the door. This one, which was supported by the figure of a unicorn carved in ivory, read: NOWHERE HOUSE.

Because she was still rather slow at reading, the door had begun to close again by the time she'd finished. She slipped hurriedly inside, and it shut behind her with a sound like muffled thunder.

Momo found herself in a long, lofty passage flanked at regular intervals by marble statues whose apparent function was to support the ceiling. There was no sign here of the mysterious current that prevailed outside in the lane. Momo followed the tortoise as it waddled ahead of her down the long corridor. At the far end it stopped outside a little door just big enough for Momo to duck through.

WE'RE HERE, the tortoise's shell announced.

There was a little sign on the door. Kneeling down so that it was on a level with her nose, Momo read the inscription. PROFESSOR SECUNDUS MINUTUS HORA, it said.

She drew a deep breath and boldly lifted the latch. As soon as the little door opened, her ears were assailed by a melodious chorus of tinkling and chiming and ticking and humming and whirring. She followed the tortoise inside, and the latch clicked into place behind them.

ELEVEN

The Conference

INNUMERABLE FIGURES were scurrying around the head-quarters of the Timesaving Bank, a gray-lit labyrinth of passages and corridors, passing on the latest news in agitated whispers: every member of the directorial board had been summoned to attend an extraordinary general meeting.

Some surmised that this portended a dire emergency, others that new and untapped sources of time had been discovered.

The directors were already closeted in the boardroom. They sat side by side at a conference table so long that it seemed to go on forever, each with his steel gray briefcase and small gray cigar. They had removed their derbies for the

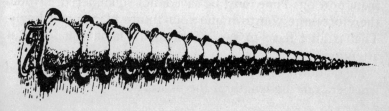

occasion, and every last one of them had a bald head as gray as the rest of him. Their mood, if such bloodless creatures could be said to have feelings at all, was universally dejected.

The chairman rose from his place at the head of the long table. The hum of conversation died away, and two interminable rows of gray faces turned toward him.

"Gentlemen," he began, "the situation is grave. I feel bound to acquaint you at once with the unpalatable but inescapable facts of the matter.

"Every available agent was assigned to hunt down the girl named Momo. This operation lasted a total of six hours, thirteen minutes, and eight seconds. While engaged on it, all the said agents were inevitably compelled to neglect the true purpose of their existence, namely, time-gathering. To this loss of revenue must be added the time expended during the manhunt by our agents themselves. Accurate computations disclose that the sum of these two debit entries amounts to three billion, seven hundred and thirty-eight million, two hundred and fifty-nine thousand, one hundred and fourteen seconds.

"That, gentlemen, is more than a whole human lifetime. I need hardly tell you what such a deficit means to us."

Here he pointed dramatically to a huge steel door, bristling with combination locks and safety devices, set in the wall at the far end of the boardroom.

"Our reserves of time are not inexhaustible, gentlemen," he pursued in a louder voice. "If the manhunt had paid off, well and good. As it is, we wasted time to no purpose. The girl eluded us.

"There must be no repetition of this disastrous affair. I shall strongly oppose any more such time-consuming operations from now on. Time must be saved, not squandered. I would therefore urge you to frame your future plans accordingly. That is all I have to say, gentlemen. Thank you for your attention."

He sat down, blowing out a dense cloud of smoke. Agitated whispers ran the length of the boardroom.

Then, at the other end of the table, a second speaker rose to his feet. Every head turned in his direction.

"Gentlemen," he said, "we all have the interests of the Timesaving Bank at heart. However, I find it quite unnecessary for us to view this affair with alarm, still less to regard it as a catastrophe. Nothing could be further from the truth. We all know that our reserves of time are so immense that our position would not be endangered, even by a loss many times greater than the one we have just sustained. What is a human lifetime, after all? By our standards, a mere pinprick.

"I fully agree with our chairman that there must be no repetition of this incident. On the other hand, nothing like it has ever happened before, and the chances of its happening again are very remote.

"The chairman was right to reproach us for allowing the girl to escape. On the other hand, our sole purpose was to render her harmless, and that we have successfully done. The creature has disappeared—she has fled beyond the borders of time. We are rid of her, in other words. Personally, I feel we have every reason to congratulate ourselves."

The second speaker sat down with a complacent smile. The smattering of applause that greeted his remarks was cut short when a third speaker rose, this time from a seat halfway along the great table.

"I shall be brief," he said sourly. "In my opinion, the last speaker's soothing words were thoroughly irresponsible. This Momo is no ordinary child. We all know she possesses powers capable of presenting a serious threat to us and our activities. We must remain on our guard. We must not rest content until the child is in our power, because only then can we be sure she will never harm us again. Having managed to leave the realm of time, she may reenter it at any moment—and she will, you mark my words!"

He sat down. The other directors winced and bowed their heads in silence.

"Gentlemen," said a fourth speaker, who was sitting across the table from the third, "pardon me for being blunt, but we're dodging the issue. We must face the fact that an alien power has been meddling in our business. After carefully examining every aspect of the situation, I find that the odds against any creature crossing the borders of time, alive and unaided, are precisely forty-two million to one. In other words, it's a near impossibility."

Another buzz of agitation ran around the boardroom.

"Everything suggests," the fourth speaker continued, when the murmurs had subsided, "that someone *helped* the girl to elude us. You all know who I mean. The person in question styles himself Professor Hora."

At the sound of this name, most of the men in gray flinched as if they had been struck. Others jumped to their feet, shouting and gesticulating.

The fourth speaker raised his arms for silence. "Gentlemen, gentlemen," he cried, "a little self-control, if you please! I'm well aware that any mention of that name is—well, not quite proper. I utter it with extreme reluctance, I assure you, but we mustn't blind ourselves to the facts. If the girl received assistance from—from the Aforesaid, he must have had his reasons, and those reasons cannot be other than detrimental to us. In short, gentlemen, we must allow for the possibility that the Aforesaid may not only send the girl back but arm her against us in some way. She will then be a mortal danger to us. We must therefore be prepared not merely to sacrifice another human lifetime or lifetimes. No, gentlemen, in the last resort we must stake everything we possess—I repeat, everything!—because, if the worst happens, thrift could spell our destruction. I think you know what I'm getting at."

The directors' agitation mounted, and they all started talking at once. A fifth speaker jumped onto his chair and waved his arms wildly.

"Quiet!" he bellowed. "It's all very well for the last speaker to hint at a host of dire possibilities, but he obviously doesn't know how to deal with them himself. He says we must be prepared for any sacrifice: well and good. We must stop at nothing: well and good. We mustn't stint our resources: well and good. But these are just empty words. Let him tell us what practical steps to take. None of us knows how the Aforesaid will arm the girl against us. We shall be confronted by a wholly unknown danger: that's the problem we have to solve!"

The boardroom was in an uproar now. Some of the directors shouted incoherently, others drummed on the table with their fists, others buried their heads in their hands. All were overcome with panic. A sixth speaker strove hard to make himself heard above the din.

"Gentlemen, please!" he kept repeating in a soothing voice until peace was finally restored. "I implore you to take a calm and commonsense view of this matter. Even assuming that the girl comes back from the Aforesaid, and even assuming that he arms her against us in some way, there will be absolutely no need for us to do battle with her ourselves. We aren't particularly well equipped for such a confrontation, as the lamentable fate of our late employee, Agent No. BLW/553/c, has so amply demonstrated. But that won't be necessary. We have human accomplices in plenty, gentlemen. Provided we make discreet and skillful use of them, we shall be able to dispose of the girl Momo and the threat she represents without ever having to intervene in person. Such a method of procedure would, I feel sure, be not only economical but safe and highly effective."

A sigh of relief went up from the assembled throng. The directors found this a sensible suggestion and would probably have adopted it on the spot had not the floor been claimed by someone seated near the head of the table.

"Gentlemen," he began, "we keep debating how best to get rid of the girl Momo. Our motive—let's be honest—is fear, but fear is a bad counselor. I feel we're missing a golden opportunity—a unique opportunity. There's a saying: If you can't beat 'em, join 'em. Well, why shouldn't we persuade the girl to join *us*? Why not get her on our side?"

"Hear, hear!" cried a number of voices. "Go on!"

"It seems clear," the seventh speaker continued, "that this child has found her way to the Aforesaid. In other words, she got there via the route that has eluded us for so long. If she can find it again, as she probably can, with ease, she can lead us there. We shall then be able to deal with the Aforesaid in our own way—very speedily, too, I feel sure.

"Once that is done, we need no longer toil at gathering time by the hour, minute, and second—no, gentlemen, because we shall have captured mankind's whole store of time at a stroke, and possessing the whole of time means wielding absolute power. Just think, gentlemen: we shall have attained our goal, and all because of the girl you propose to eliminate!"

A deathly hush had descended on the boardroom.

"That's all very well," protested someone, "but you know it's impossible to lie to the girl. Remember what happened to Agent No. BLW/553/c. We'd all end up like him."

"Who said anything about lying to her?" retorted the seventh speaker. "We'd tell her all about our plan, naturally."

"Then she'd never go along with it," the skeptic persisted. "The whole idea's preposterous."

"Don't be too sure, my friend," a ninth speaker broke in. "We'd have to make her a tempting proposition. For instance, we could promise her as much time as she wants."

"And break our promise later, of course," said the skeptic.

The ninth speaker gave an icy smile. "Of course *not,*" he said. "If we didn't mean what we said, she'd sense it at once."

"No, no!" cried the chairman, banging the table. "I couldn't agree to that. If we really gave her all the time she wanted it would cost us a fortune."

"Hardly that," the ninth speaker said blandly. "How much time can one child consume, after all? True, it would be a minor drain on our resources, but think what we'd be getting in return: the time of everyone else in the world! Momo would consume very little, and the little she did consume would simply have to be written off as overhead. Consider the advantages, gentlemen!"

The ninth speaker resumed his seat while everyone weighed the pros and cons.

"All the same," the sixth speaker said eventually, "it wouldn't work."

"Why not?"

"For the simple reason, I'm afraid, that the girl already possesses all the time she wants. There'd be no point in trying to bribe her with something she has plenty of."

"Then we'd have to deprive her of it first," the ninth speaker replied.

"We're talking in circles," the chairman said wearily. "The child's beyond our reach, that's the whole trouble."

A sigh of disappointment ran the length of the boardroom table.

"May I venture a suggestion?" asked a tenth speaker.

"The floor is yours," said the chairman.

The tenth speaker gave the chairman a little bow before proceeding. "This girl," he said, "is fond of her friends. She loves devoting her time to others. What would become of her if there were no one left to share it with her? If she won't assist us of her own free will, we must concentrate on her friends instead."

He produced a folder from his briefcase and flipped it open. "The principal persons concerned are named as Beppo Roadsweeper and Guido Guide. I also have here a list of the children who pay her regular visits. I suggest we simply lure these people away, so she can't get in touch with them. What will Momo's abundance of time amount to when she's all on her own? A burden—a positive curse! Sooner or later she won't be able to stand it anymore, and when that time comes, gentlemen, we shall present her with our terms. I'll wager a thousand years to a microsecond that she'll show us the way, just to get her friends back."

Downcast till now, the men in gray raised their heads. Every face broke into a thin-lipped smile of triumph, every pair of hands applauded. The sound reverberated along the interminable passages and corridors like an avalanche of stones rattling down a mountainside.

TWELVE

Nowhere House

MOMO WAS STANDING in the biggest room she'd ever seen. It was bigger than the biggest cathedral or concert hall in the world. Massive columns supported a roof that could be sensed rather than seen in the gloom far above. There were no windows anywhere. The golden light that wove its way across this immense hall came from countless candles whose flames burned so steadily that they looked like daubs of brilliant paint requiring no wax at all to keep them alight.

The thousandfold whirring and ticking and humming and chiming that Momo had heard on entering came from innumerable clocks of every shape and size. They reposed on long tables, in glass cabinets, on golden wall brackets, on endless rows of shelves.

There were dainty, bejeweled pocket watches, cheap tin alarm clocks, hourglasses, musical clocks with pirouetting dolls on top, sundials, clocks encased in wood and marble, glass clocks, and clocks driven by jets of water. On the walls hung all manner of cuckoo clocks and other clocks with weights and pendulums, some swinging slowly and majestically and others wagging busily to and fro. All around the room at second-floor level ran a gallery reached by a spiral staircase. Higher still was another gallery, and above it another, and above that yet another.

Clocks were standing or hanging wherever Momo looked—not only conventional clocks but spherical timepieces showing what time it was anywhere in the world, and sidereal clocks, large and small, complete with sun, moon, and stars. Arrayed in the middle of the hall were countless bigger clocks —a forest of clocks, as it were—ranging from grandfather clocks to full-size church clocks.

Not a moment passed but one of these innumerable timepieces struck or chimed somewhere or other, for each of them showed a different time. Far from offending the ear, they combined to produce a sound as pleasant and harmonious as the rustle of leaves in a wood in springtime.

Momo roamed from place to place, gazing wide-eyed at all these curiosities. She had paused beside a lavishly ornamented clock on which two tiny dancers, a man and a woman, were standing with hands entwined, and was just about to prod them to see if they would move, when she heard a friendly voice behind her. "Ah, so you're back, Cassiopeia," it said. "Did you bring Momo with you?"

Turning, Momo looked along an avenue between the grandfather clocks and saw a frail old man with silvery hair stooping over the tortoise. He was wearing a gold-embroidered frock coat, blue silk knee breeches, white hose, and shoes with big gold buckles. Lace frothed from the cuffs and collar of his coat, and his silver hair was braided into a pigtail at the back. Momo had never seen such a costume before, though anyone less ignorant would at once have recognized it as the height of fashion two centuries earlier.

"Well," said the old gentleman, still bending over the tortoise, "is she here? Where is she, then?"

He donned a small pair of eyeglasses like old Beppo's, except that these were gold-rimmed, and peered about him.

"Here I am!" called Momo.

The old gentleman came toward her with a beaming smile, both hands extended, and the nearer he drew the younger he seemed to become. By the time he had reached Momo's side, seized her hands, and shaken them cordially, he looked little older than herself.

"Welcome," he said delightedly, "—welcome to Nowhere House. Permit me to introduce myself, Momo. My name is Hora, Professor Secundus Minutus Hora."

"Were you really expecting me?" Momo asked in surprise.

"But of course. Why else would I have sent Cassiopeia to fetch you?" He produced a diamond-studded fob watch from his pocket and flipped the lid open. "In fact, you're uncommonly punctual," he said with a smile, holding out the watch for her inspection.

There were no hands or numerals on the watch face, Momo saw, just two very fine superimposed spirals rotating slowly in opposite directions. Every now and then, minute dots of light appeared where the spirals intersected.

"This watch," said Professor Hora, "is known as a crisimograph. It accurately records crises in the history of mankind, and one of these rare occurrences has just begun."

"What's a crisis?" asked Momo.

"It's like this," the professor explained. "At certain junctures in the course of existence, unique moments occur when everyone and everything, even the most distant stars, combine to bring about something that could not have happened before and will never happen again. Few people know how to take advantage of these critical moments, unfortunately, and they often pass unnoticed. When someone does recognize them, however, great things happen in the world."

"Perhaps one needs a watch like yours to recognize them by," said Momo.

Professor Hora smiled and shook his head. "No, my child, the watch by itself would be no use to anyone. You have to know how to read it as well." He snapped the watch shut and replaced it in his pocket. Then, noticing Momo's ill-concealed surprise at his personal appearance, he looked down at himself and frowned. "Ah," he said, *"you* may be punctual, but *I* seem to be rather behind the times—in fashion, I mean. How unobservant of me. I must put that right at once."

And he clicked his fingers. In a flash, his costume changed to a black frock coat, stovepipe trousers, and a stand-up collar.

"Is that any better?" he inquired doubtfully, but Momo's look of astonishment was answer enough in itself. "No, of course not," he went on quickly. "What *am* I thinking of!"

Another click of the fingers, and he instantly appeared in an outfit the like of which Momo had never seen. Nor had anyone else, since it dated from a hundred years in the future.

"Still no good?" he asked. "Never mind, I'll get it right in the end." And he clicked his fingers a third time. At long last, he stood there attired in an ordinary suit of the kind men wear today.

"That's more like it, eh?" he said, eyes twinkling. "I hope I didn't alarm you, Momo—it was just a little joke of mine. But now, my girl, come with me. You've a long journey behind you, and I'm sure you'd enjoy a hearty breakfast."

He took her by the hand and led her off into the clock forest with the tortoise following at their heels. After twisting and turning like a maze, the path eventually came out in a small room whose walls consisted of gigantic grandfather clocks. In one corner stood a bowlegged table, and beside it a dainty little sofa and some matching armchairs. Here as elsewhere, everything was bathed in the golden glow of innumerable motionless candle flames.

Set out on the table were a potbellied jug and two small cups, together with plates, spoons, and knives—all of solid, gleaming gold. There were also two little dishes, one containing golden-yellow butter, the other honey like liquid gold, and a basket piled high with crusty, golden-brown rolls. Professor Hora filled both cups with hot chocolate from the potbellied jug and made a gesture of invitation.

"There, little Momo, please help yourself."

Momo needed no second bidding. Chocolate you could

drink she'd never heard of before. As for rolls spread with butter and honey, they were a rare delicacy, and these rolls tasted more delicious than any she'd eaten in her life. Completely wrapped up in her wonderful breakfast, she feasted on it with her cheeks bulging and her mind devoid of every other thought. Although she hadn't slept a wink all night long, the food banished her weariness and made her feel fresh and lively. The more she ate, the better it tasted. She felt as if she could have gone on eating like this for days on end.

Professor Hora, who watched her benevolently, was tactful enough not to cut short her enjoyment too soon by engaging in conversation. He realized that his guest had years of hunger to make up for. Perhaps this was why, while watching her, he gradually looked older and older until he became a white-haired old gentleman again. When he noticed that Momo wasn't too handy with a knife, he spread the rolls for her and put them on her plate. He himself ate little—just enough to keep her company.

At last, even Momo could eat no more. She drank up her chocolate, studying her host over the rim of the golden cup and wondering who or what he could possibly be. He was no ordinary person, that much was obvious, but all she really knew about him so far was his name. She put her cup down and cleared her throat.

"Why did you send the tortoise to fetch me?"

"To protect you from the men in gray," Professor Hora replied gravely. "They're searching for you everywhere, and you're only safe from them here with me."

Momo looked startled. "You mean they want to hurt me?"

"Yes, my child," the professor sighed, "in a manner of speaking."

"But why?"

"Because they're afraid of you—because no one could have done them greater harm."

"I haven't done anything to them," Momo protested.

"Oh yes you have. You not only persuaded one of them to betray himself, you told your friends about him. What's more, you and your friends tried to broadcast the truth about the men in gray. Isn't that enough to make you their mortal enemy?"

"But we walked right through the city, the tortoise and I," Momo said. "If they were searching for me everywhere, they could easily have caught us. We weren't going fast."

The tortoise had stationed herself at the professor's feet. He took her on his lap and tickled her under the chin. "Well, Cassiopeia," he said with a smile, "what's your opinion? *Could* they have caught you?"

The word NEVER! appeared like lightning on Cassiopeia's shell, and the letters flickered so merrily that Momo almost thought she detected a dry little chuckle.

"The thing is," said the professor, "Cassiopeia can see into the future. Not far—just half an hour, or thereabouts—but still."

CORRECTION! flashed the shell.

"Pardon me," said the professor, "I should have said half an hour *precisely*. She knows for certain what will happen in the next thirty minutes, like whether or not she's going to bump into the men in gray, for instance."

"My goodness," exclaimed Momo, "how useful! So if she knew in advance she'd meet the men in gray at such and such a spot, would she simply take a different route?"

"No," Professor Hora replied, "I'm afraid it's not as easy as that. She can't undo anything she knows in advance because she knows what is actually going to happen. If she knew she was going to meet the men in gray at a certain spot, she'd meet them there. She'd be powerless to prevent it."

Momo's face fell. "I don't understand," she said. "In that case, there's no advantage in knowing anything in advance after all."

"There is sometimes," said the professor. "In your case, for example, she knew you were going to take a certain route and *not* meet any men in gray. That was an advantage, wasn't it?"

Momo didn't reply. Her thoughts were as tangled as a skein of wool.

"But to return to you and your friends," the professor went on. "I must congratulate you. Your posters and placards were most impressive."

"You mean you read them?" Momo asked delightedly.

"Every last word," the professor assured her.

"Nobody else did, from the look of it," said Momo.

The professor nodded sympathetically. "I'm afraid not. The men in gray saw to that."

"Do you know them well?" Momo asked.

He nodded again and sighed. "As well as they know me," he said.

Momo didn't know what to make of this reply. "Do you often go to see them?"

"No, never. I never set foot outside this house."

"What about the men in gray—do they ever come here?"

The professor smiled. "Never fear, Momo, they can't get in. They couldn't even if they knew the way to Never Lane, which they don't."

Momo thought awhile. Though reassured by Professor Hora's remarks, she was eager to learn more about him. "How do you come to know all this," she asked, "—I mean, about our posters and the men in gray."

"I keep a constant watch on them and everything connected with them," the professor told her, "so I've naturally been watching you and your friends as well."

"I thought you said you never left the house."

"I've no need to," said the professor, rapidly growing younger again as he spoke, "thanks to my omnivision glasses." He took off his little gold-rimmed spectacles and held them out. "Would you care to try them?"

Momo put them on. "I can't make out anything at all," she said, screwing up her eyes and blinking. All she could see was a whirl of colors, lights, and shadows. It made her feel positively dizzy.

"Yes," she heard the professor say, "it's always the same to begin with. Seeing through omnivision glasses isn't as easy as all that. You'll soon get used to them, though."

He stood behind Momo's chair and gently adjusted the position of the frame. At once, everything sprang into focus.

The first thing Momo saw was the men in gray and their three limousines on the edge of the district where the strange white buildings began. They were in the process of pushing their cars backward.

Then, looking farther afield, she saw more gray figures in the city streets. They were talking and gesticulating excitedly as though passing on information of some kind.

"It's you they're talking about," Professor Hora explained. "They can't understand how you managed to escape."

"Why are they all so gray in the face?" Momo asked, still watching them.

"Because they feed on dead matter," the professor told her. "They live on people's time, as you know, but time dies—literally dies—once it has been wrested away from its rightful owners. All human beings have their own share of time, but it survives only for as long as it really belongs to them."

"So the men in gray aren't human?"

"No. Their human appearance is only a disguise."

"What are they, then?"

"Strictly speaking, they're nothing."

"So where do they come from?"

"They exist only because people give them the opportunity to do so. Naturally, they seize that opportunity. Now that people are giving them a chance to rule their lives, they're naturally taking advantage of that too."

"What would happen if they couldn't steal any more time?"

"They'd disappear into thin air, which is where they come from." Professor Hora took his glasses back and pocketed them. "Unfortunately," he continued after a pause, "they already have plenty of human accomplices. That's the worst part."

"Well, nobody's going to steal any of *my* time," Momo said stoutly.

"I should hope not," said the professor. From one moment

to the next, he looked like an old man again. "Come along, Momo, I want to show you my collection."

Taking her by the hand, he led her back into the great hall, where he showed her all sorts of timepieces and made them chime for her, explained the workings of his sidereal clocks, and gradually, under the influence of his little visitor's obvious delight in all these marvels, grew younger again.

"Tell me," he said as they walked on, "do you like riddles?"

"Oh yes, very much," Momo said eagerly. "Do you know any?"

"Yes," said Professor Hora, smiling at her, "I know a real teaser. Very few people can solve it."

"All the better," Momo said. "I'll make a special note of it, so I can try it out on my friends."

The professor's smile broadened. "I can't wait to see if you solve it. Listen carefully:

> *All dwelling in one house are strange brothers three,*
> *as unlike as any three brothers could be,*
> *yet try as you may to tell brother from brother,*
> *you'll find that the trio resemble each other.*
> *The first isn't there, though he'll come beyond doubt.*
> *The second's departed, so he's not about.*
> *The third and the smallest is right on the spot,*
> *and manage without him the others could not.*
> *Yet the third is a factor with which to be reckoned*
> *because the first brother turns into the second.*
> *You cannot stand back and observe number three,*
> *for one of the others is all you will see.*
> *So tell me, my child, are the three of them one?*
> *Or are there but two? Or could there be none?*
> *Just name them, and you will at once realize*
> *that each rules a kingdom of infinite size.*
> *They rule it together and are it as well.*
> *In that, they're alike, so where do they dwell?*

Professor Hora gave Momo an encouraging nod. Thanks to her excellent memory, she was able to repeat the whole rhyme word for word. She did so, slowly and carefully, then sighed.

"Phew!" she said. "That's a really hard one. I've no idea what the answer could be. I don't even know where to start."

"Just try," said the professor.

Momo recited the riddle again under her breath. Finally, she shook her head. "It's no use," she said.

The tortoise, which had now rejoined them and was seated at the professor's feet, had been watching Momo intently.

"Well, Cassiopeia," said the professor, "you know everything half an hour in advance. Will Momo solve the riddle or won't she?"

Cassiopeia's shell lit up. SHE WILL! it spelled out.

"You see?" the professor said, turning to Momo. "You *are* going to solve it. Cassiopeia has never been wrong yet."

Momo knit her brow and racked her brains once more. Who were these three brothers that all lived in the same house? They obviously weren't brothers in the usual sense. In riddles, "brothers" always meant grains of sand or teeth or the like—similar things, at all events. But these three things somehow turned into each other. What sort of things could do that?

Looking around in search of inspiration, Momo caught sight of the candles with their motionless flames. Fire turned wax into light—yes, they were three "brothers," but that couldn't be the answer because they were all there at the same time, and two of them weren't supposed to be. What about blossom, fruit, and seed—could the answer be something of that kind? The more Momo debated this possibility, the more promising it seemed. The seed was the smallest of the three, it was there when the other two weren't, and the other two couldn't exist without it. But no, that wouldn't do either. A seed was perfectly visible, and the riddle said that anyone looking at the smallest of the three brothers always saw one of the other two.

Momo's thoughts flitted hither and thither. She simply

couldn't find a clue that led anywhere. Still, Cassiopeia had predicted that she *would* solve the riddle, so she slowly recited it to herself for a third time. When she came to the line: "The first isn't there, though he'll come beyond doubt . . ." she saw Cassiopeia give her a wink. The words WHAT I KNOW lit up on her shell, but only for a split second.

Professor Hora smiled. "No helping, Cassiopeia," he said, though he hadn't been looking in her direction. "Momo can work it out all by herself."

Momo, who had seen the words, began to ponder their meaning. What was it that Cassiopeia knew? She knew the riddle would be solved, but that was no help.

So what else did Cassiopeia know? She always knew what was going to happen. She knew . . .

"The future!" cried Momo. " 'The first isn't there, though he'll come beyond doubt'—that's the future!"

Professor Hora nodded.

" 'The second's departed,' " Momo went on, " 'so he's not about'—that must be the past!"

The professor beamed at her and nodded again.

"Now comes the hard part," Momo said thoughtfully. "What can the third brother be? He's the smallest of the three, but the other two can't manage without him, and he's the only one at home."

After another pause for thought, she gave a sudden exclamation. "Of course! It's *now*—this very moment! The past consists of moments gone by and the future of moments to come, so neither of them could exist without the present. That's it!" Her cheeks were glowing with excitement now. "But what does the next bit mean? 'Yet the third is a factor with which to be reckoned, because the first brother turns into the second . . .' I suppose it means that the present exists only because the future turns into the past."

She looked at Professor Hora with dawning amazement. "Yes, it's true! I'd never looked at it like that before. If it is true, though, there's really no such thing as the present, only past and future. Take this moment, for instance: by the time I talk about it, it's already in the past. 'You cannot stand back and observe number three, for one of the others is all you will see . . .' I understand what that means now. I understand the rest, too, because you could be forgiven for thinking there was only one brother—the present, I mean—or only the past or the future. Or none of them at all, because each of them exists only when the others do. Golly, it's enough to make your head spin!"

"But the riddle isn't finished yet," said the professor. "What's this kingdom the brothers all rule together—the one they themselves *are?*"

Momo looked baffled. What could it be? What did past, present, and future amount to, all lumped together? She gazed around the great hall, with its thousands upon thousands of clocks. Suddenly her face lit up.

"Time!" she cried, clapping her hands and skipping for joy. "That's what it is: time!"

"And the house the brothers live in—what would that be?"

"The world, I suppose," Momo replied.

"Bravo!" said the professor, clapping in his turn. "I congratulate you, my girl. You're really good at solving riddles. I'm delighted."

"Me too," said Momo, secretly wondering why he should be quite so pleased that she'd solved his riddle.

He showed her many other rare and interesting things as they resumed their tour of the clock-filled hall, but the riddle continued to occupy her thoughts.

"Tell me," she said eventually, "what exactly *is* time?"

"You've just found that out for yourself," the professor replied.

"No," she said, "I mean time itself. It exists, so it must be *something*. What is it really?"

The professor smiled. "It would be nice if you worked out your own answer to that question too."

Momo pondered for a long time. "It exists," she mused. "That much I do know, but you can't touch or hold it. Could it be something like a perfume? Then again, it's always passing by, so it must come from somewhere. Perhaps it's like the wind—no, wait! Perhaps it's a kind of music you just don't hear because it's always there." She paused, then added, "Though I have heard it sometimes, I think—very faintly."

The professor nodded. "I know, that's why I was able to summon you here."

"But there must be more to it than that," said Momo, still pursuing her train of thought. "The music comes from far off, but I seem to hear it deep inside me. Perhaps time works that way too." She broke off, bewildered. "I mean," she said, "like the wind making waves in the sea." She shrugged and shook her head. "I expect I'm talking nonsense."

"Not at all," said the professor. "I think you put it very prettily indeed. That's why I'm going to let you in on a secret. If you want to know, all the time in the world comes from here —from Nowhere House, Never Lane."

Momo gazed at him in awe. "I see," she said softly. "You mean you make it yourself?"

The professor smiled again. "No, my child, I'm merely its custodian. All human beings have their allotted span of time. My task is to see that it reaches them."

"In that case," said Momo, "why not simply arrange things so they don't have any more of it stolen by the time-thieves?"

"I can't," the professor told her. "What people do with their time is their own business. They must guard it themselves. I can only distribute it."

Momo looked around the great hall. "Is that why you keep all these clocks—one for every person in the world?"

"No, Momo, these clocks are just a hobby of mine. They're very imperfect copies of something that everyone carries inside him. Just as people have eyes to see light with and ears to hear sounds with, so they have hearts for the appreciation of time. And all the time they fail to appreciate is as wasted on them as the colors of the rainbow are wasted on a blind person or the nightingale's song on a deaf one. Some hearts are unappreciative of time, I fear, though they beat like all the rest."

"What will happen when my heart stops beating?" Momo asked.

"When that moment comes," said the professor, "time will stop for you as well. Or rather, you will retrace your steps through time, through all the days and nights, months and years of your life, until you go out through the great, round, silver gate you entered by."

"What will I find on the other side?"

"The home of the music you've sometimes faintly heard in the distance, but by then you'll be part of it. You yourself will be a note in its mighty harmonies." Professor Hora looked at Momo searchingly. "But I don't suppose that makes much sense to you, does it?"

"Yes," said Momo, "I think so." Then, recalling her strange progress along Never Lane and the way she'd lived through everything in reverse, she asked, "Are you Death?"

The professor smiled. "If people knew the nature of death," he said after a moment's silence, "they'd cease to be afraid of it. And if they ceased to be afraid of it, no one could rob them of their time anymore."

"Why not tell them, then?" Momo suggested.

"I already do," said the professor. "I tell them the meaning of death with every hour I send them, but they refuse to listen. They'd sooner heed those who frighten them. That's another riddle in itself."

"I'm not frightened," said Momo.

Professor Hora nodded slowly. He gave her another searching stare. Then he said, "Would you like to see where time comes from?"

"Yes," she whispered.

"I'll take you there," said the professor, "but only if you promise not to talk or ask questions. Is that understood?"

Momo nodded.

Professor Hora stooped and picked her up. All at once, he seemed immensely tall and inexpressibly old, but not as a man grows old—more in the manner of an ancient tree or primeval crag. Clasping Momo with one arm, he covered her eyes with his other hand, so gently that it felt as if snowflakes were landing on her cheeks like icy thistledown.

Momo sensed that he was striding down a long, dark tunnel, but she felt quite safe and utterly unafraid. At first she thought she could hear her own heartbeats, but then she became more and more convinced that they were really the echoes of the professor's footsteps.

After what seemed a very long way, he put Momo down. His face was close to hers when he removed his hand from her eyes. He gave her a meaningful look and put a finger to his lips. Then he straightened up and stepped back.

Everything was bathed in a sort of golden twilight.

When her eyes became accustomed to it, Momo saw that she was standing beneath a mighty dome as big as the vault of heaven itself, or so it seemed to her, and that the whole of this dome was made of the purest gold.

High overhead, in the very center of the dome, was a circular opening through which a shaft of light fell straight onto an equally circular lake whose dark, smooth waters resembled a jet-black mirror.

Just above the surface, glittering in the shaft of light with the brilliance of a star, something was slowly and majestically moving back and forth. Momo saw that it was a gigantic pendulum, but one with no visible means of support. Apparently weightless, it soared and swooped above the mirror-smooth water with birdlike ease.

As the glittering pendulum slowly neared the edge of the lake, an enormous water lily bud emerged from its dark depths. The closer the pendulum came, the wider it opened, until at last it lay full-blown on the surface.

Momo had never seen so exquisite a flower. It was composed of all the colors in the spectrum—brilliant colors such as Momo had never dreamed of. While the pendulum hovered above it, she became so absorbed in the spectacle that she forgot everything else. The scent alone seemed something she had always craved without knowing what it was.

But then, very slowly, the pendulum swung back, and as it did so Momo saw to her dismay that the glorious flower was beginning to wilt. Petal after petal dropped off and sank into the blackness below. To Momo, it was as if something unutterably dear to her were vanishing beyond recall.

By the time the pendulum reached the center of the lake, the flower had completely disintegrated. At that moment, however, a new bud arose near the opposite shore, and as the pendulum drew nearer Momo saw that an even lovelier blossom was beginning to unfold. She walked around the lake to inspect it more closely.

This new flower was altogether different from its predecessor. Momo had never seen such colors before, but these colors seemed richer and more exquisite by far. The petals, too, gave off a different and far more delicious scent, and the longer Momo studied them the more marvelous in every detail she found them.

But again the glittering pendulum swung back, and as it did so the glorious blossom withered and sank, petal by petal, into the dark and unfathomable depths of the lake.

Slowly, very slowly, the pendulum proceeded on its way, but not to exactly the same place as before. This time it checked its swing a little way farther along the shore, and there, one pace from where it had previously paused, another bud arose and unfolded.

To Momo this seemed the loveliest lily of all, the flower of flowers—a positive miracle. She could have wept aloud when this perfect blossom, too, began to fade and subside into the depths, but she remembered her promise to Professor Hora and uttered no sound.

Meanwhile, the pendulum had returned to the opposite shore, another pace farther along, and a fresh bud broke the glassy surface.

As time went by, it dawned on Momo that each new blossom differed entirely from those that had gone before, and that it always seemed the most beautiful of all. She wandered around the lake watching flower after flower unfold and die.

Although she felt she would never tire of this spectacle, she gradually became aware of another marvel—one that had escaped her till now: she could not only see the shaft of light that streamed down from the center of the dome; she could hear it as well.

At first it reminded her of wind whistling in distant treetops, but the sound swelled until it resembled the roar of a waterfall or the thunder of waves breaking on a rocky shore.

More and more clearly, Momo perceived that this mighty sound consisted of innumerable notes whose constant changes of pitch were forever weaving different harmonies. It was music, yet it was also something else. All at once, she recognized it as the faraway music she had sometimes faintly heard while listening to the silence of a starry night.

But now, as the sound became ever clearer and more glorious, she sensed that it was the resonant shaft of light that summoned each bud from the dark depths of the lake and fashioned it into a flower of unique and inimitable beauty.

The longer she listened, the more clearly she could make out individual voices—not human voices, but notes such as might have been given forth by gold and silver and every other precious metal in existence. And then, beyond them, as it were, voices of quite another kind made themselves heard, infinitely remote yet indescribably powerful. As they gained strength, Momo began to distinguish words uttered in a language she had never heard before but could nonetheless understand. The sun and moon and planets and stars were telling her their own, true names, and their names signified what they did and how they all combined to make each hour-lily flower and fade in turn.

Suddenly Momo realized that all these words were directed at her. From where she stood to the most distant star in space, the entire universe was focused upon her like a single face of unimaginable size, looking at her and talking to her. What overcame her then was something more than fear.

A moment later she caught sight of Professor Hora silently beckoning to her. She ran to him and buried her face in his chest. Taking her in his arms, he put one hand over her eyes as before, light as thistledown, and carried her back along the endless tunnel. Again all seemed dark, but again she felt snug and secure.

Once they were back in the little, clock-lined room, he laid her down on the sofa.

"Professor Hora," Momo whispered, "I never knew that everyone's time was so"—she strove to find the right word, but in vain—"so big," she said eventually.

"What you've just seen and heard wasn't everyone's time," the professor replied, "it was only your own. There's a place like the one you visited in every living soul, but only those who let me take them there can reach it, nor can it be seen with ordinary eyes."

"So where was I?"

"In the depths of your own heart," said the professor, gently stroking her tousled hair.

"Professor Hora," she whispered again, "may I bring my friends to see you too?"

"No," he said, "not yet. That isn't possible."

"How long can I stay with you, then?"

"Until you feel it's time to rejoin your friends, my child."

"But may I tell them what the stars were saying?"

"You may, but you won't be able to."

"Why not?"

"Because, before you can, the words must take root inside you."

"But I want to tell them—all of them. I want to sing them what the voices sang. Then everything would come right again, I think."

"If that's what you really want, Momo, you must learn to wait."

"I don't mind waiting."

"I mean, wait like a seed that must slumber in the earth before it can sprout. That's how long the words will take to grow up inside you. Is that what you want?"

"Yes," she whispered.

"Then sleep," said Professor Hora, gently passing his hand across her eyes. "Sleep!"

And Momo heaved a deep, contented sigh and fell asleep.

PART THREE

The Hour-Lilies

THIRTEEN

A Year and a Day

MOMO AWOKE and opened her eyes.

It was a while before she gathered where she was. To her bewilderment, she found herself back on the grass-grown steps of the amphitheater. If she'd been with Professor Hora in Nowhere House only moments before, how had she made her way back here so quickly?

It was cold and dark, with the first light of dawn just showing above the eastern skyline. Momo shivered and burrowed deeper into her baggy jacket.

She had a vivid recollection of all that had happened: of trudging through the city behind the tortoise, of the district with the strange glow and the dazzling white houses, of Never Lane and the great hall filled with clocks, of hot chocolate and rolls and honey, of her conversation with Professor Hora. She could even recall the riddle, word for word. Above all, though, she recalled what she had witnessed beneath the golden dome. She had only to shut her eyes to see the hour-lilies in all their undreamed-of splendor. As for the voices of the sun, moon, and stars, they still rang in her ears so clearly that she could hum the melodies they sang.

And while she did so, words took shape within her—words that truly described the scent of the flowers and the colors she had never seen before. It was the voices in her memory that spoke them, yet the memory itself brought something wonderful in its train. Momo found that she could recall not only what she had seen and heard but much, much more besides. Hour-lilies by the thousand blossomed in her mind's eye, welling up as if from some magical, inexhaustible spring, and new words rang out as each new flower appeared. Momo had only to listen closely and she could repeat the words—even sing them. They told of strange and wonderful things, but their meaning eluded her as soon as she uttered them.

So that was what Professor Hora had meant when he said that the words must first take root within her!

Or had everything been a dream after all? Had none of it really happened? Momo was still pondering this question when she caught sight of something crawling across the arena below her. It was the tortoise, engaged in a leisurely quest for edible plants.

Momo ran quickly down the steps and knelt on the ground beside it. The tortoise looked up for a moment, regarded her briefly with its dark, age-old eyes, and calmly went on eating.

"Good morning, Tortoise," said Momo.

The creature's shell remained blank.

"Was it you that took me to Professor Hora last night?"

Still no answer.

Momo heaved a sigh of disappointment. "What a pity," she muttered. "So you're only an ordinary tortoise after all, and not—oh, I've forgotten what she was called. It was a pretty name, but long and foreign-sounding. I'd never heard it before."

Some faintly luminous letters showed up on the tortoise's shell. CASSIOPEIA, they read.

Momo joyfully spelled them out. "Yes," she cried, clapping

her hands, "that was it! So it *is* you. You are Professor Hora's tortoise, aren't you?"

WHO ELSE?

"Why didn't you say so right away, then?"

HAVING BREAKFAST.

"Oh, I'm so sorry," said Momo. "I didn't mean to disturb you. All I'd like to know is, why am I back here?"

BY CHOICE.

Momo scratched her head. "That's funny, I don't remember wanting to leave. How about you, Cassiopeia? Why did you come too, instead of staying with the professor?"

BY CHOICE, Cassiopeia repeated.

"Thanks," said Momo. "That was nice of you."

NOT AT ALL. That seemed to conclude the conversation as far as Cassiopeia was concerned, because she plodded off to resume her interrupted breakfast.

Momo sat down on the steps, impatient to see Beppo, Guido, and the children again. The music continued to ring out inside her, and though she was all alone with no one around to hear, she joined in the words and melodies more and more loudly and lustily. And as she sang, straight into the rising sun, it seemed to her that the birds and crickets and trees—even the amphitheater's timeworn stones—were listening to her.

Little did she know that they would be her only listeners for a long time to come. Little did she know that she was waiting in vain for her friends to appear—that she had been gone a whole year, and that everything had changed in the meantime.

The men in gray disposed of Guido with relative ease.

It had all begun about a year ago, only days after Momo's sudden and mysterious disappearance, when a leading newspaper printed an article about him. Headlined "The Last of the Old-Time Storytellers," it mentioned when and where he could be found and described him as an attraction not to be missed.

From then on, the amphitheater was besieged by growing

numbers of people anxious to see and hear him. This, of course, was all right with Guido. He continued to say the first thing that came into his head and ended by handing around his cap, which always came back brimming with coins and bank notes. Before long he was employed by a travel agent who paid him an additional fee for permission to present him as a tourist attraction in his own right. Busloads of sightseers rolled up in such numbers that Guido was soon obliged to keep to a strict timetable, so that all who had paid to hear him got a chance to do so.

He began to miss Momo more and more, because his stories had lost their inspiration, but he steadfastly refused to tell the same story twice, even when offered twice his usual fee.

After a few months, Guido no longer needed to turn up at the amphitheater and hand around his battered peaked cap. Having been "discovered," first by a radio network and then by television, he was soon earning a mint of money by telling his stories, three times weekly, to an audience of millions.

By now he had given up his lodgings near the amphitheater and moved to quite another part of town, where all the rich and famous lived. He rented a big modern villa set in well-kept grounds, dropped the nickname Guido, and called himself Girolamo instead.

Guido was far too pressed for time, of course, to go on inventing new stories as he used to. He began to ration his material with care, sometimes concocting as many as five stories out of one idea. When even that failed to meet the ever-increasing demand for his services, he did something he should never have done: he broadcast a story destined for Momo's ears alone.

It was lapped up as greedily, and forgotten as speedily, as all the rest, and the public clamored for more. Guido was so bemused by the sheer pace of everything that, without stopping to think, he reeled off all of Momo's treasured stories in quick succession. When the last of them was told, he felt drained and empty and incapable of making up any more.

Terrified that success might desert him, he started to tell his stories all over again, making only minor changes and using different names for his characters. Extraordinarily enough, nobody seemed to notice—at all events, it didn't affect his popularity.

Guido clung to this thought like a drowning man clutching at a straw. He was rich and famous now, he told himself, and wasn't that what he'd always dreamed of?

Sometimes, though, while lying awake at night between silk sheets, he yearned for his old way of life—for the happy times he'd spent with Momo and Beppo and the children, when he was still a genuine storyteller.

But there was no way back, for Momo had never reappeared. Guido had made strenuous efforts to find her at first, but he no longer had the time. He now employed three super-efficient secretaries to negotiate contracts for him, take down his stories in shorthand, handle his publicity, and keep his engagement diary. Somehow, his schedule never left him time to resume the search for Momo.

One day, when little of the old Guido remained, he pulled what was left of himself together and resolved to turn over a new leaf. He was a somebody now, he told himself. He carried a lot of weight with millions of listeners and viewers. Who was better placed than he to tell them the truth? He would tell them about the men in gray, emphasize that the story was a true one, and ask all his fans to help him look for Momo.

He formed this intention late one night, when he had been pining for his old friends. By daybreak he was at his massive desk, preparing to put his ideas down on paper. Even before he had written a word, however, the telephone rang. He picked up the receiver, listened, and went rigid with terror. At the sound of the peculiarly flat, expressionless voice in his ear, he felt as if the very marrow in his bones had turned to ice.

"Drop the idea," the voice said. "We advise you to, for your own sake."

"Who's speaking?" Guido demanded.

"You know very well," the voice replied. "We've no need to introduce ourselves. You haven't had the pleasure of making our acquaintance, but we've owned you body and soul for a long time now. Don't pretend you didn't know."

"What do you want?"

"This latest scheme of yours doesn't appeal to us. Be a good boy and drop it, will you?"

Guido took his courage in both hands. "No," he said, "I won't. I'm not poor little Guido Guide any longer, I'm a celebrity. Try taking me on and see how far you get!"

The voice gave such a gray, mirthless laugh that Guido's teeth began to chatter.

"You're a nobody," it said, "—a rubber doll. We've blown you up, but give us any trouble and we'll let the air out. Do you seriously think you owe what you are today to yourself and your own unremarkable talents?"

"Yes," Guido said hoarsely, "that's just what I do think."

"Poor old Guido," said the voice, "you're still as much of a dreamer as you ever were. You used to be Prince Girolamo disguised as a nobody called Guido. And what are you now? Just a nobody called Guido disguised as Prince Girolamo. You should be grateful to us. After all, we're the ones who made your dreams come true."

"That's a lie!" Guido shouted.

"Heavens!" said the voice with another mirthless laugh. "You're hardly the person to bandy words with us on the subject of truth and falsehood. Oh no, my poor Guido, you'll regret it if you try quoting the truth at people. Thanks to us, you've become famous for your tall stories. You aren't qualified to tell the truth, so forget it."

"What have you done with Momo?" Guido asked in a whisper.

"Don't worry your poor little scatterbrained head about that. You can't help her anymore, least of all by telling stories about us. If you do, you'll only destroy your success as quickly as it came. It's up to you, of course. If you're really set on playing the hero and ruining yourself, we won't stop you, but you can't expect us to reward your ingratitude by continuing

to protect your interests. Don't you like being rich and famous?"

"Yes," Guido replied in a muffled voice.

"Exactly, so leave us out of it. Go on telling people what
they want to hear."

"Now that I know the truth," Guido said with an effort,
"how can I?"

"I'll give you some sound advice: don't take yourself so
seriously. The matter's out of your hands. Look at it from that
angle and you'll find you can carry on very nicely, as before."

"Yes," Guido muttered, staring into space, "from that angle . . ."

The earpiece gave a click and went dead. Guido hung up
too. He slumped forward onto the desktop and buried his face
in his arms, racked with silent sobs.

From then on Guido lost every last scrap of self-respect. He
abandoned his plan and carried on as before, though he felt
an utter fraud. And so he was. Once upon a time his imagination had soared along and he had blithely followed its lead,
but now he was telling lies. He was making a buffoon of
himself—a public laughingstock—and he knew it. He hated
his work, and the more he hated it the sillier and more senti-
mental his stories became. This didn't impair his reputation,
though. On the contrary, the public acclaimed him for pio-
neering a new style of humor and many comedians tried to
imitate it. Guido was all the rage, not that he derived any
pleasure from the fact. He now knew who was responsible for
his success. He had gained nothing and lost everything.

And still he continued to race by car or plane from one
engagement to the next, accompanied everywhere by the secretaries to whom he never stopped dictating old stories in new
guises. "Amazingly inventive" was the newspapers' pet
description of him.

Guido the dreamer had, in fact, become Girolamo the
hoaxer.

Beppo Roadsweeper presented the men in gray with a far harder nut to crack.

Ever since the night of Momo's disappearance, and whenever his work permitted, he had gone to the amphitheater and sat there waiting. At last, when his mounting concern and anxiety became too much to bear, he resolved to override Guido's objections, reasonable though they were, and go to the police.

"What if they do put her back in one of those homes with bars over the windows?" he reflected. "Better that than being held prisoner by the men in gray—if she's still alive, of course. She escaped from a children's home once, so she could do it again. Besides, maybe I could fix it so they didn't put her in a home at all. The first thing to do is find her."

So he made his way to the nearest police station, which was on the outskirts of the city. Once there, he hung around outside for a while, twisting his hat in his hands. Then he plucked up courage and walked in.

"Yes?" said the desk sergeant, who was busy filling out a long and complicated form.

Beppo took some time to get it out. "The thing is," he said at last, "something dreadful must have happened."

"Really?" said the desk sergeant, still writing. "What's it all about?"

"It's about our Momo," said Beppo.

"A child?"

"Yes, a girl."

"Is she yours?"

"No," Beppo said uncertainly, "—I mean, yes, but I'm not her father."

"No, I mean, yes!" snapped the desk sergeant. "Who's child is she, then? Who are her parents?"

"Nobody knows," said Beppo.

"Where is she registered, then?"

"Registered?" said Beppo. "Well, with us, I suppose. We all know her."

"So she *isn't* registered," the desk sergeant said with a sigh.

"That's against the law, in case you didn't know. Who does she live with, then?"

"She lives by herself," Beppo replied, "that's to say, she used to live in the old amphitheater, but she doesn't anymore. She's gone."

"Just a minute," said the desk sergeant. "If I understand you correctly, the ruins have until recently been occupied by a young female vagrant named—what did you say her name was?"

"Momo," said Beppo.

The policeman pulled a pad toward him and started writing. "Momo," he repeated. "Well, go on: Momo what? I'll need her full name."

"Momo nothing," said Beppo. "Just Momo."

The desk sergeant stroked his chin and looked aggrieved. "See here, old-timer, you'll have to do better than this. I'm trying to be helpful, but I can't file a report without your cooperation. Better begin by telling me your own name."

"Beppo," said Beppo.

"Beppo what?"

"Beppo Roadsweeper."

"Your name, I said, not your occupation."

"It's both," Beppo explained patiently.

The desk sergeant put his pen down and buried his face in his hands. "God give me strength!" he muttered despairingly. "Why did I have to be on duty now, of all times?"

Then he straightened up, squared his shoulders, and gave the old man an encouraging smile. "All right," he said gently, as though humoring a child, "I can take your personal particulars later. Just tell me the whole story from start to finish."

Beppo looked dubious. "All of it?"

"Anything that's relevant," said the desk sergeant. "I'm up to my eyes in work—I've got this whole stack of forms to complete by lunchtime, and I'm just about at the end of my tether—but never mind that. Take your time and tell me what's on your mind."

He sat back and closed his eyes with the air of a martyr at

the stake. And Beppo, in his queer, roundabout way, recounted the whole story from Momo's arrival on the scene and her exceptional gifts to the trial on the garbage dump, which he himself had witnessed.

"And that very same night," he concluded, "Momo disappeared."

The desk sergeant subjected him to a long, resentful glare. "I see," he said at last. "So you're telling me that an unlikely-sounding girl, whose existence remains to be proved, may have been kidnapped and carried off, you can't say where to, by ghosts of some kind. Is that what you expect us to investigate?"

"Yes, please," Beppo said eagerly.

The desk sergeant leaned forward. "Breathe on me!" he barked.

Although Beppo failed to see the point of this request, he shrugged his shoulders and obediently blew in the policeman's face.

The desk sergeant sniffed and shook his head. "You don't appear to be drunk."

"No," mumbled Beppo, puce in the face with embarrassment. "I've never been drunk in my life."

"Then why tell me such a cock-and-bull story? Did you really think I'd be daft enough to believe it?"

"Yes," Beppo replied innocently.

At that the policeman's patience finally snapped. He jumped up and slammed his fist down hard on his stack of long and complicated forms. "That does it!" he bellowed, beside himself with rage. "Get out of here at once or I'll lock you up for insulting behavior!"

Beppo looked dismayed. "I'm sorry," he mumbled, "I didn't mean it that way. All I meant was—"

"Out!" roared the desk sergeant.

Beppo turned and went.

During the next few days he called at various other police stations with much the same result. He was thrown out, politely sent home, or humored as the best means of getting rid of him.

One day, however, he was interviewed by a police inspector with less sense of humor than his colleagues. After listening to Beppo's story without a flicker of expression, he turned to a subordinate and said coldly, "The old man's off his rocker. We'll have to find out if he's a threat to society. Take him down to the cells."

Beppo had to spend half the day in a cell before being whisked off in a car by two policemen. They drove him all the way across the city to a big white building with bars over the windows. It wasn't a prison or detention center, as he at first thought, but a hospital for nervous disorders.

Here Beppo underwent a thorough examination. The hospital staff treated him kindly. They didn't laugh at him or bawl him out—in fact they seemed very interested in his story, because they made him tell it again and again. Although they never questioned it, Beppo got the feeling that they didn't really believe it. Whatever they made of him, which was far from clear to Beppo himself, they didn't discharge him.

Whenever he asked how soon he could go, he was told, "Soon, but you're still needed for the time being. We haven't completed our investigations, but we're making progress." And Beppo, who thought they were referring to investigations into Momo's whereabouts, continued to wait patiently.

They had allotted him a bed in a big ward where many other patients slept. One night he woke up and saw, by the feeble glow of the emergency lighting, that someone was standing beside his bed. All he could tell at first was that the shadowy figure was smoking a cigar or cigarette—the tip glowed red in the gloom—but then he recognized the derby and briefcase. Realizing that his visitor was one of the men in gray, he felt chilled to the marrow and opened his mouth to call for help.

"Quiet!" hissed an ashen voice. "I've been authorized to make you a proposition. Listen to it carefully, and don't answer till I tell you. You now have some idea of the power we already wield. Whether or not you get another taste of it is entirely up to you. Although you can't harm us in the least by retailing your story to all and sundry, it doesn't suit our scheme of things. You're quite correct in assuming that your friend Momo is our prisoner, but you may as well abandon all hope of finding her. That you'll never do, and your efforts to rescue her aren't making the poor girl's position any easier. Every time you try, *she* has to suffer for it, so be more careful what you do and say from now on."

The man in gray blew several smoke rings, gleefully observing the effect of his speech on Beppo. It was clear that the old man believed every word of it.

"My time is valuable," the man in gray went on, "so here's our proposition in a nutshell: you can have the girl back, but only on condition that you never utter another word about us or our activities. As ransom, so to speak, we shall additionally require you to deposit a hundred thousand hours of your time with us. How we bank it is our affair and doesn't concern you. All you have to do is save it. How you save it is *your* affair. If you agree, we'll arrange for you to be released in the next few days. If not, you'll stay here for as long as Momo remains with us, in other words, for evermore. It's a generous offer, so think it over. You won't get a second chance. Well?"

Beppo swallowed hard a couple of times. Then he croaked, "I agree."

"Very sensible of you," the man in gray said smugly. "So remember: absolute discretion and a hundred thousand hours of your time. As soon as you've saved them for us, you can have Momo back. And now, my dear sir, goodbye."

On that note the man in gray departed, leaving a trail of cigar smoke behind him. It seemed to glow faintly in the darkness like a will-o'-the-wisp.

Beppo stopped telling his story from that night on, and when asked why he'd told it in the first place would merely look sad and shrug his shoulders. The hospital authorities discharged him a few days later.

But he didn't go home. Instead, he went straight to the depot where he and his fellow workers collected their brooms and handcarts. Shouldering his broom, he marched out into the city streets and started sweeping.

He did not, however, sweep as he used to in the old days, with a breath before each step and stroke of the broom, but hurriedly and without pride in his work, solely intent on saving time. He felt sickened by what he was doing and tormented by the knowledge that he was betraying the deeply held beliefs of a lifetime. Had no one's future been at stake but his own, he would have starved to death rather than abandon his principles, but there was Momo's ransom to collect, and this was the only way he knew of saving time.

He swept day and night without ever returning to his shack near the amphitheater. When exhaustion overcame him, he would sit down on a park bench, or even on the curb, and snatch a few minutes' sleep, only to wake up with a guilty start and carry on sweeping. He devoted just as little time to his meals, which took the form of hurried snacks wolfed down on the move.

Beppo swept for weeks and months on end. Winter followed autumn, and still he toiled on. Spring and summer came around, but he scarcely noticed the changing seasons. Preoccupied with saving Momo's hundred thousand hours' ransom, he swept and swept and swept.

The townsfolk were too short of time themselves to pay any attention to the little old man, and the handful that did so tapped their foreheads as soon as he had gone panting past, wielding his broom as if his life depended on it. Being taken for a fool was nothing new to Beppo, so he scarcely noticed that either. On the few occasions when someone asked him what the hurry was, he would pause for a moment, eye the questioner with mingled alarm and sorrow, and put his finger to his lips.

Hardest of all for the men in gray to tailor to their plans were Momo's friends among the children of the city. Even after her disappearance, they went on meeting at the amphitheater as often as they could. They continued to invent new games in which a few old crates and boxes became castles and palaces or galleons that carried them on fabulous voyages around the world. They also continued to tell each other stories. In short, they behaved as if Momo were still with them, and by doing so, remarkably enough, they almost made it seem that she really was.

Besides, they never for a moment doubted that she would return. They didn't discuss the subject, but children united by such an unspoken certainty had no need to. Momo was one of them and formed the ever-present focus of all their activities, whether or not she was actually there in person.

The men in gray were powerless to meet this challenge head-on. Unable to detach the children from Momo by bringing them under their direct control, they had to find some roundabout means of achieving the same end, and for this they enlisted the children's elders. Not all grown-ups made suitable accomplices, of course, but there were plenty that did. What was more, the men in gray were smart enough to turn the children's own weapons against them.

Quite suddenly, one or two parents recalled how their offspring had paraded through the streets with placards and posters.

"Something must be done," they said. "More and more kids are being left on their own and neglected. You can't blame us—parents just don't have the time these days—so it's up to the authorities."

Others joined in the chorus. "We can't have all these youngsters loafing around," declared some. "They obstruct traffic. Accidents caused by children are on the increase, and accidents cost money that could be put to better use."

"Unsupervised children run wild," declared others. "They become morally depraved and take to crime. The authorities must take steps to round them up. They must build centers where the youngsters can be molded into useful and efficient members of society."

"Children," declared still others, "are the raw material of the future. A world dependent on computers and nuclear energy will need an army of experts and technicians to run it. Far from preparing our children for tomorrow's world, we still allow too many of them to squander years of their precious time on childish tomfoolery. It's a blot on our civilization and a crime against future generations."

The timesavers were all in favor of such a policy, naturally, and there were so many of them in the city by this time that they soon convinced the authorities of the need to take prompt action.

Before long, big buildings known as "child depots" sprang up in every neighborhood. Children whose parents were too busy to look after them had to be deposited there and could be collected when convenient. They were strictly forbidden to play in the streets or parks or anywhere else. Any child caught doing so was immediately carted off to the nearest depot, and its parents were heavily fined.

None of Momo's friends escaped the new regulation. They were split up according to the districts they came from and consigned to various child depots. Once there, they were naturally forbidden to play games of their own devising. All games were selected for them by supervisors and had to have some useful, educational purpose. The children learned these new games but unlearned something else in the process: they forgot how to be happy, how to take pleasure in little things, and, last but not least, how to dream.

Weeks passed, and the children began to look like timesavers in miniature. Sullen, bored, and resentful, they did as they were told. Even when left to their own devices, they no longer knew what to do with themselves. All they could still do was make a noise, but it was an angry, ill-tempered noise, not the happy hullabaloo of former times.

The men in gray made no direct approach to them—there was no need. The net they had woven over the city was so close-meshed as to seem impenetrable. Not even the smartest and most ingenious children managed to slip through it. The amphitheater remained silent and deserted.

The men in gray had done their work well. All was in readiness for Momo's return.

So Momo sat on the stone steps and waited in vain for her friends to turn up. She sat and waited all day, but no one came —not a soul.

The sun was sinking in the west. The shadows grew longer, the air more chill.

At last Momo rose stiffly to her feet. She was hungry because no one had thought to bring her something to eat. This had never happened before. Even Guido and Beppo must have forgotten about her, she reflected, but she consoled herself with the thought that it was just an oversight—a silly mistake that would sort itself out the next day.

She went and knelt beside the tortoise, which had already tucked itself in for the night. Timidly, she tapped the shell with her knuckles. The tortoise put its head out and looked at her.

"Excuse me," Momo said, "I apologize for waking you, but can you tell me why none of my friends came? I waited all day long."

ALL GONE, the shell spelled out.

Momo read the words but couldn't follow their meaning. "Oh well," she said cheerfully, "I'll find out tomorrow. My friends are bound to come then, aren't they?"

NEVER AGAIN, replied the tortoise.

Momo stared at the faint letters with growing dismay. "What do you mean?" she asked eventually. "Has something happened to them?"

ALL GONE, she read again.

She shook her head. "No," she said softly, "they can't have. You must be wrong, Cassiopeia. Why, I saw them only yesterday at our grand council of war—the one that came to nothing."

NOT YESTERDAY, Cassiopeia replied.

Momo remembered now. Professor Hora had told her that she would have to wait like a seed slumbering in the earth until it was ready to sprout. She had agreed without stopping to wonder how long that meant, but now the truth was beginning to dawn on her.

"How long have I been away?" she asked in a whisper.

A YEAR AND A DAY.

Momo took some time to digest this. "But Beppo and Guido," she stammered, "—surely *they're* still waiting for me?"

NO ONE LEFT, she read.

"But I don't understand." Momo's lips were trembling. "They can't all be gone, not my friends, not the times we spent together . . ."

Very slowly, a single word lit up on Cassiopeia's shell: PAST.

For the first time in her life, Momo grasped the terrible finality of the word. Her heart had never felt so heavy.

"But," she murmured helplessly, "—but *I'm* still here . . ." She longed to cry but couldn't. A moment later she felt the tortoise nudge her bare foot.

SO AM I, she read.

"Yes," she said, smiling bravely, "you're here too, Cassiopeia, and I'm glad of your company. Come on, let's go to bed."

Picking up the tortoise, she carried it through the hole in the wall and down into her room. She saw by the light of the setting sun that all was just as she had left it—Beppo had tidied the place up after its invasion by the men in gray—but everything was thick with dust and shrouded in cobwebs.

Then she caught sight of an envelope propped against a can on the little table. The envelope, too, was covered with cobwebs. *"To Momo,"* it said.

Momo's heart began to race. No one had ever written her a letter before. She picked up the envelope and examined it from every angle, then tore it open and unfolded the slip of paper inside.

"Dear Momo," she read, *"I've moved. If you come back, please get in touch with me at once. I miss you and worry about you a lot. I hope nothing has happened to you. If you're hungry, go to Nino's place. I'll*

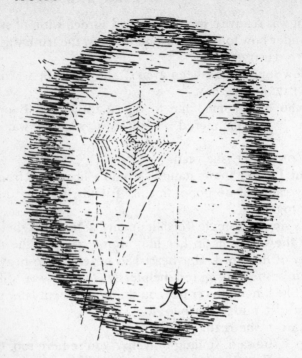

foot the bill, so be sure to eat as much as you want. Nino will tell you the rest. Keep on loving me—I still love you. Yours ever, Guido."

Momo took a long time to decipher this letter, even though Guido had obviously been at pains to write as neatly and legibly as possible. The daylight had gone by the time she finished reading, but she felt comforted.

She took the tortoise and put it on the bed beside her. "You see, Cassiopeia," she said as she wrapped herself in the dusty blanket, "I'm not alone after all."

But the tortoise seemed to be asleep already, and Momo, who had pictured Guido's face with the utmost clarity while reading his letter, never suspected that the envelope had been lying there for almost a year.

She pillowed her cheek on it, feeling cold no longer.

FOURTEEN

Three Lunches, No Answers

TOWARD NOON on the following day, Momo tucked the tortoise under her arm and set off for Nino's inn.

"You'll see, Cassiopeia," she said. "The mystery will soon be solved. Nino will tell us where Guido and Beppo are. Then we'll go and get the children, and we'll all be together again. Perhaps Nino and his wife will come along too. You'll like my friends, I'm sure. We could even give a little party this evening. I'll tell everyone about the flowers and the music and Professor Hora and everything. Oh, I just can't wait to see them all again! First, though, I'm looking forward to a good lunch. I'm absolutely famished."

And so she chattered on merrily, feeling in her jacket pocket now and then to reassure herself that Guido's letter was still there. The tortoise fixed her with its wise old eyes and made no comment.

Momo began to hum as she went, and then to sing. The words and melodies were those of the voices that still seemed to ring in her ears as clearly as they had the day before. She would never forget them, she knew that now.

Then, abruptly, she broke off. They had reached Nino's inn, but her first thought was that she must have gone astray. Where once had stood a little old tavern with damp-stained walls and a vine growing around the door, the street was flanked by a long, concrete box with big plate glass windows. The street itself had been asphalted and was humming with traffic. A big gas station had sprung up opposite, and alongside it an enormous office building. There were lots of cars parked outside the new establishment, and the neon sign above the entrance said: NINO'S FAST FOOD.

Momo went inside. She found it hard to get her bearings at first. Cemented into the floor beside the windows were a number of tables with such spindly single legs and tiny tops that they looked like toadstools. They were just the right height for grown-ups to eat at standing up—which was fortunate, since there were no chairs.

Running along the other side of the room was a sort of fence made of shiny, chromium-plated tubing. Just beyond it stood a long row of glass cases containing ham and cheese sandwiches, sausages, plates of salad, puddings, cakes, and countless other things to eat, many of which Momo had never seen before.

She could only take in the scene by degrees because the room was jam-packed with people, and she always seemed to be getting in their way. No matter where she stood, they elbowed her aside or jostled her along. Most of them were balancing trays laden with food and drink, and all were intent on grabbing a place at one of the little tables. Behind every man or woman that stood there, eating in frantic haste, several others waited impatiently for him or her to finish. From time to time, acrimonious remarks were exchanged by those eating and those still waiting to eat. All of them looked glum and discontented.

More people were shuffling slowly along behind the barrier, taking plates or bottles and cardboard cups from the glass cases as they passed.

Momo was astonished. So they could help themselves to

whatever they liked! There was no one around to stop them or ask them to pay for what they took. Perhaps everything was free, Momo reflected. That would certainly account for the crush.

At last she spotted Nino. Almost obscured by customers, he was seated in front of a cash register at the very end of the long row of glass cases, pressing buttons, taking money, and giving change without a stop. So he was the person who took the money! The rail fenced people in so they couldn't get to the tables without passing him.

"Nino!" she called, trying to squeeze through the crowd. She called again and waved Guido's letter, but Nino didn't hear. The electronic cash register was bleeping too loudly.

Plucking up her courage, Momo climbed over the rail and wormed her way along the line to where Nino sat. He glanced up, because one or two customers had started to protest. At the sight of Momo, his glum expression disappeared in a flash.

"So you're back!" he exclaimed, beaming just as he used to in the old days. "This *is* a nice surprise!"

"Get a move on," called an angry voice. "Tell that kid to stand in line like the rest of us. Cheeky little brat, barging her way to the front like that!"

Nino made appeasing gestures. "I won't be a moment," he said. "Be patient, can't you?"

"Anyone could jump the line at this rate," another voice chimed in. "Hurry it up, we don't have as much time to spare as she does."

"Look, Momo," Nino whispered hurriedly, "take whatever you like—Guido will pay for it all—but you'll have to line up like the rest. You heard what they said."

Before Momo could reply, she was pushed past the cash register by the people behind her. There was nothing for it but to do as the others did. Joining the end of the line, she took a tray from a shelf and a knife, fork, and spoon from a box. Because she needed both hands for the tray, she dumped Cassiopeia on top.

Rather flustered by now, Momo took things at random from the glass cases as she was slowly propelled along, step by step, and arranged them around the tortoise. She ended up with an oddly assorted meal: a piece of fried fish, a cream puff, a sausage, a meat pie, and a plastic mug of lemonade. Surrounded by food on all sides, Cassiopeia retired into her shell without comment.

When Momo at last reached the cash register, she hurriedly asked Nino if he knew where Guido was.

Nino nodded. "Our Guido's a celebrity these days. We're all very proud of him—he's one of us, after all. He's on TV and radio every week, and they're always writing about him in the papers. I even had two reporters here myself last week, asking about the old days. I told them how Guido used to—"

"Move along in front!" called an irate voice.

"But why doesn't he come around anymore?" Momo asked.

"Ah well," Nino muttered, fidgeting because his customers were making him nervous, "he doesn't have the time, you see. He's got more important things on his mind. Besides, there's nothing doing at the amphitheater, not now."

"What's the matter with you?" called another indignant voice. "You think we *like* hanging around here, or something?"

Momo dug her heels in. "Where's Guido living now?" she asked.

"Somewhere on Green Hill," Nino replied. "He's got a fine house there, so they say, with a great big garden—but please, Momo, do me a favor and come back later!"

Momo didn't really want to move on—she had a lot more questions for him—but someone shoved her in the back again. She took her tray to one of the toadstool tables and actually managed to get a place, though the table was so high that her nose was on a level with it. When she slid the tray on top, the neighboring grown-ups eyed Cassiopeia with disgust.

"Ugh! See the kind of thing we have to put up with nowadays?" someone said to the person beside him, and the other man growled, "What do you expect? These kids!"

They left it at that and ignored Momo from then on. Eating was quite a problem because she could scarcely see what was on her tray, but being very hungry she devoured every last morsel. Then, in her anxiety to discover what had become of Beppo, she rejoined the line. Although she wasn't hungry anymore, she was so afraid people might get angry with her if she simply stood there that she filled her tray with another assortment of things from the glass cases.

"Where's Beppo?" she asked, when she finally made it back to the cash register.

"He waited for you for ages," Nino said hurriedly, fearful of upsetting his customers again. "He thought something terrible had happened to you—kept on talking about men in gray, or something of the kind. Well, you know old Beppo—he always was a bit eccentric."

"You, there!" called a voice from the back of the line. "When are we going to get some service?"

"Right away, sir!" Nino called back.

"What happened then?" asked Momo.

"Then he started pestering the police," Nino went on, nervously massaging his brow. "He asked them to look for you—made a real nuisance of himself, apparently. Next thing we knew, they'd put him in a sort of sanitarium. That's all I can tell you."

"Hell and damnation!" someone else bellowed. "Is this a fast-food joint or a dentist's waiting room? What are you doing, holding a family reunion?"

"Yes, kind of," Nino said apologetically.

"Is he still there?" asked Momo.

Nino shook his head. "I don't think so. I'm told they pronounced him harmless and let him go."

"So where is he now?"

"I've no idea, Momo, honestly I haven't. Now please be a good girl and move on."

Again Momo was jostled past the cash register by the people behind her, and again she waited for a place at one of the toadstool tables. She polished off her second trayful of food with a good deal less gusto than the first, but food was food, and she wouldn't have dreamed of leaving any.

She still had to find out what had become of the children who used to keep her company. There was nothing for it but to stand in line once more, shuffle past the glass cases, and load her tray with food rather than invite hostile remarks. It seemed an eternity before she reached the cash register again.

"What about the children?" she demanded. "What's become of them?"

"Oh, that's all changed," said Nino, breaking out in a sweat at her reappearance. "I can't explain right now—you can see how rushed I am."

"But why don't they come anymore?" she insisted.

"Nowadays, kids with no one to look after them are put in child depots. They aren't allowed to be left to themselves anymore because—well, the long and the short of it is, they're taken care of."

"Hurry it up, you slowpokes!" came an indignant chorus. "We'd like to eat sometime!"

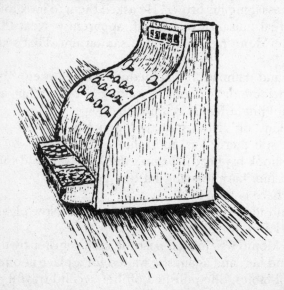

Momo was looking incredulous. "Child depots," she repeated. "Is that what my friends really wanted?"

"They weren't consulted," said Nino, fiddling with the keys of his cash register. "It's not up to kids to decide these things for themselves. Child depots keep them off the streets—that's the main thing, isn't it?"

Momo said nothing, just looked at him, and Nino squirmed under her searching gaze.

"Damn it all!" shouted yet another angry voice in the background. "This is the limit! If you must hold a prayer meeting, hold it somewhere else!"

"What am I going to do now," Momo asked in a small voice, "without my friends?"

Nino shrugged and kneaded his hands together. "Be reasonable, Momo," he said, drawing a deep breath. "Come back some other time. I really can't discuss your problems now. You're welcome to eat here any time you like, you know that, but if I were you I'd report to one of these child depots. They'd look after you and keep you occupied—they'd even give you a proper education. Besides, you'll end up in one anyway, if you go on wandering around on your own like this."

Momo said nothing, just gazed at him as before. When the crowd swept her along she mechanically went to one of the tables and just as mechanically forced herself to eat a third lunch, though it was all she could do to get it down. It tasted so much like cardboard and wood shavings, she felt sick.

Then, tucking Cassiopeia under her arm, she walked silently to the door without a backward glance.

"Hey, Momo!" called Nino, who had spotted her at the last moment. "Wait a bit! You never told me where you've been all this time!"

But the next customer was already drumming his fingers on the cash register. Nino rang up the total, took the man's money, and gave him some change. The smile had long since left his face.

"I've had loads to eat," Momo told Cassiopeia when they were back at the amphitheater. "Far too much, to tell the truth, but somehow I still feel empty inside." After a while she added, "Anyway, I couldn't have told Nino about the flowers and the music—there wasn't time, and I don't think he'd have understood." There was another pause before she went on, "Never mind, tomorrow we'll go and look for Guido. You're sure to like him, Cassiopeia, believe me."

But all that lit up on Cassiopeia's shell was a great big question mark.

FIFTEEN

Found and Lost

MOMO GOT UP EARLY the next morning and set off in search of Guido's house. Cassiopeia came too, of course.

Momo knew where Green Hill was. A residential suburb several miles from the amphitheater, it lay on the other side of the city, near the housing development's identical rows of identical apartment houses.

Green Hill was a long walk. Although Momo was used to going without shoes, her bare feet were aching by the time she got there, so she sat down on the curb to rest awhile.

It really was a very smart neighborhood. The streets were broad and clean and deserted. In gardens enclosed by high walls and iron railings, fine old trees reared their branches to the sky. Most of the houses set in these gardens were long, low, flat-roofed villas built of concrete and glass. The smooth expanses of lawn in front of them were lush and green—they positively cried out for children to turn somersaults on them —but not a soul could be seen strolling or playing anywhere. Presumably the owners didn't have time.

Momo turned to Cassiopeia. "If only I knew how to find out where Guido lives," she sighed.

YOU WILL, the tortoise signaled.

"You really think so?" Momo said hopefully.

"Hey, you grubby little brat," someone said behind her, "what are you doing here?"

Momo turned to see a man in a spotless white jacket. She didn't know that such jackets were worn by the servants of the rich. "Good morning," she said, getting up off the curb, "I'm looking for Guido's house. Nino told me he lives here now."

"*Whose* house?"

"Guido's. He's a friend of mine, you see."

The man in the white jacket glared at her suspiciously. He had left the garden gate ajar, and Momo could see inside. Some dogs were frisking around on a big stretch of lawn, and a fountain was playing in front of the house. Overhead, in a blossom-covered tree, perched a pair of peacocks.

"Oh," Momo exclaimed, "what pretty birds!" She started to go inside for a closer look, but the man in the white jacket grabbed her by the scruff of the neck.

"No, you don't!" he said. "Some nerve you've got, I must say." Then he let go of her and wiped his fingers on his handkerchief, looking as if he'd just touched something unpleasant.

Momo pointed through the gate. "Does all that belong to you?" she inquired.

"No," snapped the man in the white jacket, sounding more unfriendly than ever. "And now, clear off. You've no business here."

"Oh yes I have," Momo said firmly. "I've got to find Guido Guide. He's expecting me. Don't you know him?"

"There aren't any guides around here," the man retorted, and turned on his heel. He had gone back into the garden and was about to slam the gate when a thought seemed to strike him.

"You don't mean Girolamo, the TV star?"

"That's right," Momo said eagerly. "Guido Guide—that's his real name. Can you tell me which his house is?"

"Is he really expecting you?" the man demanded.

"Yes, truly he is," said Momo. "He's a friend of mine—he pays for everything I eat at Nino's."

The man in the white jacket raised his eyebrows and shook his head. "These showbiz people," he said acidly, "they certainly get some crazy notions sometimes. All right, if you really think he'll welcome a visit from you, his house is right at the end of the street."

So saying, he slammed the gate behind him.

The word SHOW-OFF appeared on Cassiopeia's shell, but only for a moment.

The last house in the street was surrounded by a high wall, and the gate was made of sheet metal like all the rest, so it was impossible to see inside. There wasn't a nameplate or a doorbell anywhere in sight.

"Can this really be Guido's new house?" said Momo. "It doesn't look at all the kind of place he'd choose."

IT IS, Cassiopeia signaled.

"But why is it all shut up?" Momo asked. "I'll never get in."

WAIT, was Cassiopeia's advice.

Momo sighed. "I may have to wait a long time. Even if Guido's home, how will he know I'm here?"

The tortoise's shell lit up again. HE'LL COME, it said.

So Momo sat down, right outside the gate, and waited patiently. Nothing happened for such a long time that she began to wonder if Cassiopeia had made a mistake for once.

"Are you absolutely positive?" she asked after a while.

Cassiopeia's reply was quite unexpected. Her shell said simply, GOODBYE.

Momo gave a start. "What do you mean, Cassiopeia? You aren't leaving me, are you? Where are you going?"

TO LOOK FOR YOU, was Cassiopeia's still more cryptic response.

At that moment the gate swung open without warning and out shot a long, low, elegant car. Momo, who jumped back only just in time, fell head over heels. The car sped on for several yards, then screeched to a halt. An instant later, Guido jumped out.

"Momo!" he cried, flinging his arms wide. "If it isn't my own, beloved little Momo!"

Momo scrambled to her feet and ran to him, and Guido snatched her up in his arms and covered her cheeks with kisses and danced around in the roadway with her.

"Did you hurt yourself?" he asked breathlessly, but instead of waiting for a reply he went on talking a blue streak. "Sorry I gave you a fright, but I'm in a tearing hurry. Late again, as usual. Where have you been all this time? You must tell me the whole story. I'd given you up for lost, you know. Did you get my letter? Yes? So it was still there, eh? Fine, so you went and had a meal at Nino's, did you? Did you enjoy it? Oh, Momo, we've such a lot to tell each other—so much has happened in the last few months. How are you, anyway? What's the matter, lost your tongue? And what about old Beppo—what's he up to these days? I haven't seen him in a month of Sundays. And the children—what about them? Oh, Momo, I can't tell you how often I think of the times we spent together, when I used to tell you stories. Good times they were, but everything's different now—you can't imagine how different."

Momo had made several attempts to answer his questions, but since his torrent of words never dried up she simply watched and waited. Guido looked different from the old days. He was well-groomed and he smelled nice, but there was something curiously unfamiliar about him.

Meanwhile, some people had emerged from the limousine and walked over to them: a man in a chauffeur's uniform and three hard-faced, heavily made-up young women.

"Is the child hurt?" asked one, sounding less anxious than disapproving.

"No, no, not a bit," Guido assured her. "We gave her a fright, that's all."

"Serves her right for loitering outside the gate," said the second young woman.

Guido laughed. "But this is Momo—my old friend Momo!"

The third young woman raised her eyebrows. "So she really exists, does she? I always thought she was a figment of your imagination. We must issue a press release at once. 'Girolamo Reunited with His Fairy Princess'—something along those lines. I'll get onto it at once. What a story! The public will lap it up."

"No," said Guido, "I'd rather not."

"What do *you* say, Momo?" asked the first young woman, fixing Momo with an artificial smile. "Surely *you'd* like to see your picture in the paper, wouldn't you?"

"Leave her alone!" snapped Guido.

The second young woman glanced at her wristwatch. "We're going to miss our flight if we don't get a move on, and you know what that would mean."

"God almighty," Guido protested, "can't I even have a quiet chat with a long-lost friend?" He turned to Momo with a rueful grin. "You see? They never give me a moment's peace, these slave drivers of mine—never."

"Suit yourself, but we're only doing our job," the second young woman said tartly. "That's what you pay us for, lord and master, to arrange your schedule and see that you stick to it."

Guido gave in. "Okay, okay, we'd better get going. Tell you what, Momo, why not come to the airport with us? We can talk on the way, and afterward my chauffeur will drive you home, all right?"

Without even waiting for an answer, he seized Momo's hand and towed her to the car. The three secretaries got in behind while Guido sat up front with Momo squeezed in beside him.

"Right," he said, "I'm listening, but first things first. How come you disappeared like that?"

Momo was on the point of telling him about Professor Hora and the hour-lilies when one of the secretaries leaned forward.

"Sorry to butt in," she said, "but I've just had the most

fabulous idea. We've simply *got* to introduce Momo to the top brass at Fantasy Films Inc. She'd be perfect for the name part in your next movie—the one about the girl who becomes a hobo. Think what a sensation it would make: 'Momo, starring as Momo!' "

"Didn't you hear what I said?" snapped Guido. "I don't want her dragged into anything of the kind, is that clear?"

The young woman bridled. "I just don't get it," she said. "Most people would jump at such a heaven-sent opportunity."

"Well, I'm not most people!" Guido shouted in a sudden fury. He turned to Momo. "Forgive me, you may not understand this, but I don't want these vultures sinking their talons into you as well as me."

At that, all three secretaries sniffed and looked offended.

Guido groaned aloud and clutched his head. Producing a small silver pillbox from his pocket, he took out a capsule and gulped it down.

Nobody spoke for a minute or two.

At length Guido turned to the trio behind him. "I apologize," he mumbled wearily, "I wasn't referring to you. My nerves are on edge, that's all."

"We know," said the first young woman, "we're getting used to it."

"And now," Guido went on, smiling down at Momo rather wryly, "lets's not talk about anything except the two of us."

"One more question before it's too late," the second young woman broke in. "We'll be there any minute. Couldn't you at least let me do a quick interview with the kid?"

"That's enough!" roared Guido, beside himself with rage. "I want a word with Momo in private—it means a lot to me. How many more times do I have to tell you?"

The second young woman was just as irate. "You're always complaining because the publicity I get you doesn't pack a big enough punch."

"You're right," Guido groaned, "but not now. Not *now!*"

"It's too bad," the second young woman pursued. "A human interest story like this would be a real tearjerker, but have it your way. Maybe we can run it later on, when—"

"No!" Guido cut in. "Neither now nor later—not ever! Now kindly shut up while Momo and I have a talk."

"Well, pardon *me!*" the second young woman retorted angrily. "It's your publicity we're discussing, not mine. Think carefully: Can you really afford to pass up such an opportunity at this stage in your career?"

"No, I can't," Guido cried in desperation, "but Momo stays out of it! And now, for pity's sake, leave us in peace for five minutes."

The secretaries relapsed into silence. Limply, Guido drew a hand across his eyes.

"You see how far gone I am?" He patted Momo's arm and gave a wry little laugh. "I couldn't go back now, even if I wanted to—I'm beyond redemption. 'Guido's still Guido!'— remember? Well, Guido isn't Guido anymore. Believe me, Momo, there's nothing more dangerous in life than dreams that come true, at least when they come true like mine. I've nothing left to dream about, and not even you could teach me to dream again. I'm fed up to the teeth with everything and everyone."

He stared morosely out of the window.

"The most I could do now would be to stop telling stories and keep mum, if not for the rest of my life, at least until people had forgotten all about me and I was poor and unknown again. But poverty without dreams? No, Momo, that would be sheer hell. I'd sooner stay where I am. That's another kind of hell, but at least it's a comfortable one." Guido broke off. "I don't know why I'm rambling on like this. You can't have understood a word."

Momo just looked at him. What she understood, first and foremost, was that Guido was ill—gravely ill. She suspected that the men in gray were at the bottom of it, but she had no idea how to cure him if he didn't want to be cured.

"I've done nothing but talk about myself," he said. "It's high time you told me about your own doings."

Just then the car drew up outside the airport terminal. They all got out and hurried into the concourse, where a pair of uniformed stewardesses were already waiting for Guido. Some newspaper reporters took pictures of him and asked questions, but the stewardesses started fussing because there were only a few minutes left before takeoff time.

Guido bent down and gazed into Momo's eyes, and suddenly his own eyes filled with tears.

"Listen," he said, lowering his voice so the others couldn't hear. "Stay with me, Momo. I'll take you along on this trip— I'll take you wherever I go. You can live in that fine new house of mine and dress in silk and satin like a real princess. Just be there and listen to me, that's all I ask. If you did, perhaps I'd manage to think up some proper stories like the ones I used to tell, know what I mean? Just say yes, Momo, and everything will be all right again. Help me, I beg you!"

Momo's heart bled for Guido. She longed so much to help him, but she sensed that he was wrong. He would have to become Guido again, and it wouldn't help him at all if she stopped being Momo. Her eyes, too, filled with tears, and she shook her head.

Guido understood. He just had time to nod sadly before he was hustled off by the three secretaries he employed to do just that. He gave one last wave in the distance, and Momo waved back. Then he was hidden from view.

Momo could have told him so many things, but she hadn't managed to say a word throughout their brief reunion. She felt as if, by finding him again, she had really and truly lost him at last.

Slowly, she turned and made her way across the crowded concourse. Just as she reached the exit, she was smitten by a sudden thought: she had lost Cassiopeia as well!

SIXTEEN

Loneliness

"WHERE TO?" asked the chauffeur when Momo got in beside him.

She looked perplexed. Where *did* she want to go? She had to look for Cassiopeia, but where? Where had she lost her? The tortoise hadn't been with them on the drive to the airport, that much she knew for sure, so the likeliest place would be outside Guido's house. Then she remembered the words on Cassiopeia's shell: GOODBYE and TO LOOK FOR YOU. Of course! Cassiopeia had known beforehand that they would lose each other, so she'd gone looking for her. But where should she, Momo, go looking for Cassiopeia?

"Make up your mind," said the chauffeur, beating an impatient tattoo on the steering wheel. "I've got better things to do with my time than take you joyriding."

"Back to Guido's house, please," Momo replied.

The chauffeur looked faintly surprised. "I thought the boss said to drive you home. You mean you're coming to live at his place?"

"No," said Momo, "but I lost something in the road outside, and I've got to find it."

That suited the chauffeur, who had to go back there anyway. As soon as they reached Guido's gate, Momo got out and started peering in all directions.

"Cassiopeia!" she called softly, again and again. "Cassiopeia!"

The chauffeur stuck his head out of the window. "What are you looking for?"

"Professor Hora's tortoise," Momo told him. "Her name is Cassiopeia, and she always knows what's going to happen half an hour in advance. She can make words light up on her shell, too—that's how she tells you what the future holds in store. I've simply got to find her. Would you help me to look for her, please?"

"I've no time for jokes," snarled the chauffeur, and drove on. The remote-controlled gate opened and closed behind him.

Undaunted, Momo continued the search on her own. She combed the entire street, but Cassiopeia was nowhere to be seen.

"Perhaps she's on her way back to the amphitheater," thought Momo, so she slowly retraced her steps, calling the tortoise by name all the way. She peered into every nook and cranny, every ditch and gutter, but in vain.

Although Momo didn't get back to the amphitheater till late that night, she searched it as thoroughly as the darkness would allow. She had nursed a vague hope that Cassiopeia might, by some miraculous means, have reached home before her, but she knew in her heart of hearts that the tortoise's slow rate of progress rendered this impossible.

At long last she crept into bed, really alone for the first time ever.

Once she had given Cassiopeia up for lost, Momo decided to concentrate on trying to find Beppo. She spent the next few weeks roaming aimlessly through the city in search of him. No one could give her any clue to his whereabouts, so her one remaining hope was that they might simply bump into each other. The vastness of the city made this a forlorn hope. They had as little chance of meeting as a shipwrecked sailor has that his message in a bottle will be netted by a fishing boat ten thousand miles from the desert island where he tossed it into the sea.

For all that, Momo kept telling herself, she and Beppo might be quite close to each other. Who could tell how often she had passed some spot where he had been only an hour, a minute, or even a moment or two before? Conversely, how often had Beppo crossed a square or rounded a street corner only minutes or moments after her? Encouraged by this thought, Momo often waited in the same spot for hours. She had to move on sooner or later, however, so even that was no insurance against their missing each other by a hair's breadth.

How useful Cassiopeia would have been! The tortoise could have signaled WAIT! or KEEP GOING! As it was, Momo never knew what to do for the best. She was afraid of missing Beppo if she waited, and just as afraid of missing him if she didn't.

She also kept her eyes open for the children who used to come and play with her in the old days, but she never saw a single one. She never saw any children at all, though this was hardly surprising in view of Nino's remark about their being "taken care of."

Momo herself was never picked up by a policeman or other adult and taken off to a child depot, for the very good reason that she was under constant surveillance by the men in gray. She didn't know it, but confinement to a child depot wouldn't have suited their plans for her.

Although she ate at Nino's restaurant every day, she never managed to say any more to him than she had on the first occasion. He was always in just as much of a rush and never had the time.

Weeks became months, and still Momo pursued her solitary existence. One evening, while perched on the balustrade of a bridge, she sighted the small, bent figure of a man on another bridge in the distance, wielding a broom as if his life depended on it. Momo shouted and waved, thinking it was Beppo, but the man didn't stop work for an instant. She ran as fast as she could, but by the time she reached the other bridge there was no one in sight.

"I don't suppose it was him," she told herself consolingly. "No, it can't have been. I know the way Beppo works."

Some days she stayed home at the amphitheater on the off chance that Beppo might look in to see if she was back. If she was out when he came, he would naturally assume that she was still away. It tormented her to think that this might already have happened a week or even a day ago, so she waited —in vain. Eventually she painted the words I'M BACK on the wall of her room in big, bold letters, but hers were the only eyes that ever saw them.

The one thing that never forsook Momo in all this time was her vivid recollection of Professor Hora, the hour-lilies, and the music. She had only to shut her eyes and listen to her heart, and she could see the blossoms in all their radiant splendor and hear the voices singing. And even though the words and melodies were forever changing, she found she could repeat the words and sing the melodies as easily as she had on the very first day. Sometimes she spent whole days sitting alone on the steps, talking and singing to herself with no one there to hear but the trees and the birds and the timeworn stones.

There are many kinds of solitude, but Momo's was a solitude few people ever know and even fewer experience with such intensity. She felt as if she were imprisoned in a vault heaped with priceless treasures—an ever-growing hoard that threatened to crush the life out of her. There was no way out, either. The vault was impenetrable, and she was far too deeply buried beneath a mountain of time to attract anyone's attention.

There were even moments when she wished she had never heard the music or seen the flowers. And yet, had she been offered a choice, nothing in the world would have induced her to part with her memories of them, not even the prospect of death. Yes, death, for she now discovered that there are treasures capable of destroying those who have no one to share them with.

Every few days, Momo made the long walk to Guido's house and waited outside the gate for hours in the hope of seeing him again. By now she was ready to agree to anything—ready to stay with him and listen to him, whether or not things became as they once were—but the gate remained firmly shut.

Only a few months passed in this way, yet Momo had never lived through such an eternity. No clock or calendar can truly measure time, just as no words can truly describe the loneliness that afflicted her. Suffice it to say that if she had succeeded in finding her way back to Professor Hora—and she tried to again and again—she would have begged him to cut off her supply of time or let her remain with him at Nowhere House for evermore.

But she couldn't find the way without Cassiopeia's help, and Cassiopeia, whether long since back with Professor Hora or lost and roaming the big, wide world, had never reappeared.

Instead, something quite different happened.

While wandering through the city one day, Momo ran into Paolo, Franco, and Maria, the girl who always used to carry her little sister Rosa around with her. All three children had changed so much she hardly recognized them. They were dressed in a kind of gray uniform, and their faces wore a strangely stiff and lifeless expression. They barely smiled, even when Momo hailed them with delight.

"I've been looking for you for so long," she said breathlessly. "Will you come back to the amphitheater and play with me?"

The three children looked at each other, then shook their heads.

"But you'll come tomorrow, won't you, or the next day?"

Again the trio shook their heads.

"Oh, do come!" Momo pleaded. "You always used to in the old days."

"In the old days, yes," said Paolo, "but everything's different now. We aren't allowed to fritter our time away."

"We never did," Momo protested.

"It was nice," Maria said, "but that's not the point."

And the three of them hurried on with Momo trotting beside them.

"Where are you off to?" she asked.

"To our play class," Franco told her. "That's where they teach us how to play."

Momo looked puzzled. "Play what?"

"Today we're playing data retrieval," Franco explained. "It's a very useful game, but you have to concentrate like mad."

"How does it go?"

"We all pretend to be punch cards, and each card carries various bits of information about us—age, height, weight, and so on. Not our real age, height, and weight, of course, because that would make it too easy. Sometimes we're just long strings of letters and numerals, like MUX/763/Y. Anyway, then we're shuffled and fed into a card index, and one of us has to pick out a particular card. He has to ask questions in such a way that all the other cards are eliminated and only the right one is left. The winner is the person who does it quickest."

"Is it fun?" Momo asked, looking rather doubtful.

"That's not the point," Maria repeated uneasily. "Anyway, you shouldn't talk like that."

"So what is the point?" Momo insisted.

"The point is," Paolo told her, "it's useful for the future."

By this time they had reached a big, gray building. The sign over the gate said CHILD DEPOT.

"I had so much to tell you," Momo said.

"Maybe we'll see each other again sometime," Marie said sadly.

As they stood there, more children appeared. They

streamed in through the gateway, all looking just the same as Momo's former playmates.

"It was much nicer playing with you," Franco said suddenly. "We used to enjoy thinking up games for ourselves, but our supervisors say they didn't teach us anything useful."

"Couldn't you just run away?" Momo hazarded.

The trio shook their heads and glanced around for fear someone might have overheard.

"I tried it a couple of times at the beginning," Franco whispered, "but it's hopeless. They always catch you again."

"You shouldn't talk like that," said Maria. "After all, we're taken care of now."

They all fell silent and stared gloomily into space. At last Momo summoned up her courage and said, "Couldn't you take me in with you? I'm so lonely these days."

Just then, something extraordinary happened. Before the

children could reply they were whisked into the courtyard of
the building like iron filings attracted by a giant magnet, and
the gates clanged shut behind them.

After a minute, when she had recovered from her shock,
Momo cautiously approached the gates intending to knock or
ring and beg to be allowed to join in, no matter what game the
children were playing. She had barely taken a couple of steps,
however, when she stopped dead, rooted to the spot with
terror. A man in gray had suddenly materialized between her
and the gates.

"Pointless," he said with a thin-lipped smile, the inevitable
cigar jutting from the corner of his mouth. "Don't even try it.
Letting you in would be against our interests."

"Why?" Momo asked. She felt as if her limbs were slowly
filling with ice water.

"Because we have other plans for you," said the man in
gray, blowing a smoke ring that coiled itself around her neck
and took a long time to disperse.

People were passing by, all in too much of a hurry to give
them a second glance. Momo pointed to the man in gray and
tried to call for help, but no sound escaped her lips.

"Save it," said the man in gray with a bleak, mirthless laugh.
"You ought to know us better than that—you know how powerful we are. No one can help you, now we've got all your
friends. You're at our mercy too, but we've decided to go easy
on you."

"Why?" Momo managed to get out.

"Because we'd like you to do us a little favor. Be sensible,
and you can do yourself and your friends a lot of good. What
do you say?"

"All right," whispered Momo.

The man in gray gave another thin-lipped smile. "Then
we'll meet at midnight to talk it over."

She nodded mutely, but the man in gray had already vanished. All that marked the spot where he had stood was a wisp
of cigar smoke.

He hadn't told her where they were to meet.

SEVENTEEN

The Square

MOMO WAS TOO SCARED to go back to the amphitheater. She felt sure the man in gray would turn up there for their midnight meeting, and the thought of being all alone with him in the deserted ruins filled her with terror.

No, she never wished to see him again, neither there nor anywhere else. Whatever his proposition might be, it boded no "good" for her and her friends—that was as plain as the nose on your face. But where could she hide from him?

A crowded place seemed the best bet. Although no one had taken any notice before, if the man in gray really tried to harm her and she called for help, people would surely hear and come to her aid. Besides, she told herself, she'd be harder to find in a crowd than on her own.

So Momo spent the rest of the afternoon walking the busiest streets and squares surrounded by jostling pedestrians. All through the evening and well into the night she continued to trudge in a big circle that brought her back to her starting point. Around and around she went, swept along by a fast-flowing tide of humanity, until she had completed no fewer than three of these circuits.

After keeping this up for so many hours, her weary feet began to ache. It grew later and later, but still she walked, half asleep, on and on and on . . .

"Just a little rest," she told herself at last, "—just a teeny little rest, and then I'll be more on my guard . . ."

Parked beside the curb was a little three-wheeled delivery truck laden with an assortment of sacks and cartons. Momo climbed aboard, found herself a nice, soft sack, and leaned her back against it. She drew up her weary feet and tucked them under her skirt. My, did that feel good! She heaved a sigh of relief, snuggled up against the sack, and was asleep before she knew it.

But she was haunted by the weirdest dreams. In one of them she saw old Beppo, with his broom held crossways like a balancing pole, teetering along a tightrope suspended above a dark chasm. "Where's the other end?" she heard him call, over and over again. "I can't see the other end!" And the tightrope did indeed seem infinitely long—so long that it stretched away into the darkness in both directions. Momo yearned to help the old man, but she couldn't even attract his attention; he was too high up and too far away.

Then she saw Guido, pulling a paper streamer out of his mouth. He pulled and pulled, but the streamer was endless and unbreakable—in fact he was already standing on a big mound of paper. It seemed to Momo that he was gazing at her imploringly, as if he would suffocate unless she came to his rescue. She tried to run to him, but her feet became entangled in the coils of paper, and the more she struggled to free herself the more entangled she became.

And then she saw the children. They were all as flat as playing cards, and each card had a pattern of little holes punched in it. Every time the cards were shuffled they had to sort themselves out and be punched with a new pattern of holes. The card children were crying bitterly, but all Momo could hear was a sort of clattering sound as they were shuffled yet again and fluttered down on top of each other. "Stop!" she shouted, but her feeble voice was drowned by the clatter, which grew louder and louder until it finally woke her up.

It was dark, and for a moment she couldn't think where she was. Then she remembered climbing aboard the delivery truck and realized that it was on the move. That was what had woken her—the sound of the engine.

Momo wiped her cheeks, which were still wet with tears, and wondered where she could be. The truck had evidently been on the move for some time, because it was in a different part of the city. At this late hour not a soul could be seen in the streets, not a light showed anywhere in the tall buildings that flanked them.

The truck was going quite slowly, and Momo, without stopping to think, jumped out. She began walking in the opposite direction, eager to get back to the crowded streets that seemed to offer protection from the man in gray. Then, remembering her nightmares, she came to a halt.

The sound of the engine gradually faded until silence enveloped the darkened street.

She would stop running away, Momo decided. She had done so in the hope of saving herself. All this time she had been preoccupied with herself, her own loneliness and fear, when it was really her friends who were in trouble. If anyone could save them, she could. Remote as the chances of persuading the men in gray to release them might be, she must at least try.

Once she reached this conclusion, she felt a mysterious change come over her. Her feelings of fear and helplessness had reached such a pitch that they were suddenly transformed into their opposites. Having overcome them, she felt courageous and self-confident enough to tackle any power on earth; more precisely, she had ceased to worry about herself.

Now she *wanted* to meet the man in gray—wanted to at all costs.

"I must go to the amphitheater at once," she told herself.

"Perhaps it still isn't too late, perhaps he'll be waiting for me."

That, however, was easier said than done. She didn't know where she was and hadn't the least idea which direction to take, but she started walking anyway.

On and on she walked through the dark, silent streets. Being barefoot, she couldn't even hear her own footsteps. Every time she turned a corner she hoped to see something that would tell her she was on the right track, some landmark she recognized, but she never did. She couldn't ask the way, either, because the only living creature she saw was a grimy, emaciated dog that was foraging for scraps in a garbage heap and fled in panic at her approach.

At last she came to a huge, deserted square. It wasn't a handsome square with trees or a fountain in the middle, but an empty, featureless expanse fringed with buildings whose dark shapes stood outlined against the night sky.

Momo set off across the square. When she reached the middle, a clock began to chime not far away. It chimed a good many times, so perhaps it was already midnight. If the man in gray was waiting for her at the amphitheater, Momo reflected, she had no chance at all of getting there in time. He would go away without seeing her, and any chance of saving her friends would be gone, perhaps forever.

She chewed her knuckles, wondering what to do. She had absolutely no idea.

"Here I am!" she called into the darkness, as loud as she could. She had no real hope that the man in gray would hear her, but she was wrong.

Scarcely had the last chime died away when lights appeared in all the streets that led to the big, empty square, faint at first but steadily growing brighter—drawing nearer. And then Momo realized that they were the headlights of innumerable cars, all converging on the spot where she stood. Dazzled by the glare no matter which way she turned, she shielded her eyes with her hand. So they were coming after all!

But Momo hadn't expected them to come in such strength. For a moment, all her newfound courage deserted her. Hemmed in and unable to escape, she shrank as far as she could into her baggy old jacket.

Then, remembering the hour-lilies and the mighty chorus of voices, she instantly felt comforted. The strength flowed back into her limbs.

Meanwhile, with their engines purring softly, the cars had continued their slow advance. At last they stopped, bumper to bumper, in a circle whose central point was Momo herself.

The men in gray got out. Momo couldn't see how many of them there were because they remained outside the ring of headlights, but she sensed that many eyes were on her—unfriendly eyes—and a shiver ran down her spine.

No one spoke for a while, neither Momo nor any of the men in gray. Then a flat, expressionless voice broke the silence.

"I see," it said. "So this is Momo, the girl who thought she could defy us. Just look at her now, the miserable creature!"

These words were followed by a dry, rattling sound that vaguely resembled a chorus of mocking laughter.

"Careful!" hissed another gray voice. "You know how dangerous she can be. It's no use trying to deceive her."

Momo pricked up her ears at this.

"Very well," said the first voice from the darkness beyond the headlights, "let's try the truth for a change."

Another long silence fell. Momo sensed that the men in gray were afraid to tell the truth—so afraid that it imposed a tremendous strain on them. She heard what sounded like a gasp of exertion from a thousand throats.

At long last, one of the disembodied voices began to speak.

It came from a different direction, but it was just as flat and expressionless as the others.

"All right, let's be blunt. You're all on your own, little girl. Your friends are out of reach, so you've no one to share your time with. We planned it that way. You see how powerful we are. There's no point in trying to resist us. What do they amount to, all these lonely hours of yours? A curse and a burden, nothing more. You're completely cut off from the rest of mankind."

Momo listened and said nothing.

"Sooner or later," the voice droned on, "you won't be able to endure it any longer. Tomorrow, next week, next year—it's all the same to us. We shall simply bide our time because we know that in due course you'll come crawling to us and say: I'll do anything, anything at all, as long as you relieve me of my burden. But perhaps you've already reached that stage? You only have to say."

Momo shook her head.

"So you won't let us help you?" the voice pursued coldly. Momo felt an icy breeze envelop her from all sides at once, but she gritted her teeth and shook her head again.

"She knows what time is," whispered another voice.

"That proves she really was with a Certain Person," the first voice replied, also in a whisper. Aloud, it asked, "Do you know Professor Hora?"

Momo nodded.

"You actually paid him a visit?"

She nodded again.

"So you know about the hour-lilies?"

She nodded a third time. Oh yes, how well she knew!

There was another longish silence. When the voice began to speak again, it came from another direction.

"You love your friends, don't you?"

Another nod.

"And you'd like to set them free?"

Yet another nod.

"You could, if only you would."

Momo was shivering with cold in every limb. She drew the jacket more tightly around her.

"It wouldn't take much to save them. You help us and we'll help you. That's only fair, isn't it?"

The voice was coming from yet another direction. Momo stared intently at its source.

"The thing is, we'd like to make Professor Hora's acquaintance but we don't know where he lives. All we want is for you to show us the way. That's right, Momo, listen carefully, so you know we're being honest with you and mean what we say. In return, we'll give you back your friends and let you all lead the carefree, happy-go-lucky life you used to enjoy so much. If that isn't a worthwhile offer, what is?"

Momo opened her mouth for the first time. It was quite an effort to speak at all, her lips felt so numb.

"What do you want with Professor Hora?" she asked.

"I told you, we want to make his acquaintance," the voice said sharply, and the air grew even colder. "That's all you need to know."

Momo said nothing, just waited.

"I don't understand you," said the voice. "Think of yourself and your friends. Why worry about Professor Hora? He's old enough to look after himself. Besides, if he's sensible and cooperates nicely, we won't harm a hair of his head. If not, we have ways of making him."

Momo's lips were blue with cold. "Making him do what?" she asked.

The voice sounded suddenly shrill and strained. "We're tired of collecting people's time by the hour, minute, and second. We want all of it right away, and Hora's got to hand it over!"

Horrified, Momo stared into the darkness beyond the ring of headlights. "What about the people it belongs to?" she asked. "What will happen to them?"

"People?" The voice rose to a scream and broke. "*People* have been obsolete for years. They've made the world a place where there's no room left for their own kind. *We* shall rule the world!"

By now the cold was so intense that Momo could barely move her lips, let alone speak.

"Never fear, though, little Momo," the voice went on, abruptly becoming gentle and almost coaxing, "that naturally won't apply to you and your friends. You'll be the last and only people on earth to play games and tell stories. As long as you stop meddling in our business, we'll leave you in peace. Is it a deal?"

The voice fell silent. A moment later, it took up the thread from a different quarter. "You know we've told you the truth. We'll keep our promise, you can rely on that. And now, take us to Professor Hora."

Momo tried to speak, almost fainting with cold. Finally, after several attempts, she said, "Even if I could, I wouldn't."

"What do you mean, *if* you could?" the voice said menacingly. "Of course you can. You paid him a visit, so you must know the way."

"I'd never find it again," Momo whispered. "I've tried. Only Cassiopeia knows it."

"Who's Cassiopeia?"

"The professor's tortoise."

"Where is it now?"

Momo, barely conscious, murmured, "She . . . she came back with me, but . . . I lost her."

As if from a long way off, a chorus of agitated voices came to her ears.

"Issue a general alert!" she heard. "We've got to find that tortoise. Check every tortoise you come across. That animal's got to be found at all costs!"

The voices died away. Silence fell. Momo slowly regained her senses. She was standing by herself in the middle of the square. Nothing was stirring but a chill gust of wind that seemed to issue from some great, empty void: a wind as gray as ashes.

EIGHTEEN

The Pursuit

MOMO DIDN'T KNOW how much time had passed. The church clock chimed occasionally, but she scarcely heard it. Her frozen limbs took ages to thaw out. She felt numb and incapable of making decisions.

How could she go home to the amphitheater and climb into bed, now that there was no hope left for herself and her friends? How could she, when she knew that things would never come right again? She was worried about Cassiopeia, too. What if the men in gray found her? She began to reproach herself bitterly for having mentioned the tortoise at all, but she'd been too dazed to think straight.

"Anyway," she reflected, trying to console herself, "Cassiopeia may have found her way back to Professor Hora long ago. Yes, I hope she isn't still looking for me. It would be better for both of us."

At that moment something nudged her bare foot. Momo gave a start and looked down.

There was Cassiopeia, as large as life, and she could dimly

see some words on the animal's shell: HERE I AM AGAIN, they said.

Without a second thought, Momo grabbed the tortoise and stuffed it under her jacket. Then she straightened up and peered in all directions, fearful that some men in gray might still be lurking in the shadows, but all was quiet.

Cassiopeia kicked and struggled fiercely in an effort to escape. Holding her tight, Momo peeped inside the jacket and whispered, "Please keep still!"

WHY ALL THE FUSS? demanded Cassiopeia.

"You mustn't be seen!" Momo hissed.

The next words to appear on the tortoise's shell were, AREN'T YOU GLAD?

"Of course," Momo said with a catch in her voice. "Of course I am. You've no idea!" And she kissed Cassiopeia on the nose, several times in quick succession.

Cassiopeia responded with a rather pink word. STEADY! it read.

Momo smiled. "Have you been looking for me all this time?"

OF COURSE.

"But how did you happen to find me here and now?"

I KNEW I WOULD, was the laconic reply.

Had Cassiopeia spent all those weeks looking for her although she knew she wouldn't find her? If so, she needn't really have bothered to look at all. This was yet another of Cassiopeia's little mysteries. They made Momo's head spin if she thought about them too hard, and besides, this was scarcely the moment to puzzle over such problems.

Momo gave the tortoise a whispered account of what had happened since last they met. "What should we do now?" she concluded.

Cassiopeia had been listening attentively. GO TO HORA, she spelled out.

"Now?" Momo exclaimed, aghast. "But they're looking for you everywhere. This is the only place they don't happen to be. Wouldn't it be wiser to stay here?"

But all the tortoise's shell said was, WE'RE GOING ANYWAY.

"We'll run right into them," Momo protested.

WON'T MEET A SOUL, was Cassiopeia's response.

If Cassiopeia was sure, that settled it. Momo put her down. Then, remembering their first long, arduous trek, she suddenly felt too exhausted to repeat it all over again.

"You go on alone, Cassiopeia," she said wearily. "I'm too tired. Go on alone, and give the professor my love."

Cassiopeia's shell lit up again. IT'S NOT FAR, Momo was astonished to read. It dawned on her, as she looked around, that this shabby and desolate-looking neighborhood might be the one that led to the district with the white houses and the strange shadows. If so, she might after all be able to make it as far as Never Lane and Nowhere House.

"All right," she said, "I'll come too, but wouldn't it be quicker if I carried you?"

AFRAID NOT, Cassiopeia replied.

"Why should you insist on crawling there by yourself?" Momo said, but all she got was the engimatic reply: THE WAY'S INSIDE ME.

On that note the tortoise set off with Momo following slowly, step by step.

They had only just disappeared down a side street when the shadows around the square came to life and the air was filled with a brittle sound like the snapping of dry twigs: the men in gray were chuckling triumphantly. Some of their number, who had stayed behind to keep a surreptitious watch on Momo, had witnessed her reunion with Cassiopeia. The wait had been a long one, but not even they had dreamed that it would yield such results.

"There they go!" whispered one gray voice. "Shall we nab them?"

"Of course not," hissed another. "Let them carry on."

"Why?" demanded the first voice. "Our orders were to capture the tortoise at all costs."

"Yes, but why do we want it?"

"So it can lead us to Hora."

"Precisely, that's just what it's doing now. We won't even have to use force. It's showing us the way of its own free will—unintentionally."

Another dry chuckle went up from the shadows around the square.

"Pass the word at once. Call off the search and instruct all agents to join us here. Tell them to exercise the utmost care, though. None of us must be seen by our two unsuspecting guides or get in their way. They're to be given free passage wherever they go. And now, gentlemen, let's follow at our leisure."

It was hardly surprising, under these circumstances, that Momo and Cassiopeia failed to encounter a single one of their pursuers. Whichever way they went, the men in gray melted away in good time and joined the rear of the ever-growing procession that was silently, cautiously, following in the fugitives' wake.

Momo was wearier than she had ever been in her life. There were times when she thought she would simply sink to the ground and fall asleep at any moment, but she forced herself to put one foot before the other, and for a while things went better. If only Cassiopeia wouldn't crawl along at such a snail's pace, she thought, but it couldn't be helped. She trudged along, looking neither right nor left, only at her feet and the tortoise.

After an eternity, or so it seemed to Momo, the surface of the street grew suddenly paler. She wrenched her leaden eyelids open and looked around.

Yes, they had finally reached the district where the light was neither that of dawn nor dusk, and where all the shadows ran in different directions. There were the forbidding white houses with the cavernous black windows, and there was the peculiar, egglike monument on its black stone plinth.

At the thought that it wouldn't be long before she saw

Professor Hora again, Momo's courage revived. "Please," she said to Cassiopeia, "couldn't we go a bit faster?"

MORE HASTE LESS SPEED, came the reply, and the tortoise crawled on even more slowly than before. Yet Momo noticed, as she had the first time, that they made better progress that way. It was as if the street beneath them glided past more quickly the slower they went.

That, of course, was the secret of the district with the snow-white houses: the slower you went the better progress you made, and the more you hurried the slower your rate of advance. The men in gray hadn't known that when they pursued Momo in their cars, which was how she'd escaped them.

But that was the last time. Things were quite different now that they had no intention of overtaking the girl and the tortoise. Now, because they were trailing them at exactly the same speed, they had discovered the secret. Gradually, the streets behind Momo and Cassiopeia became filled with an army of men in gray. And as the pursuers grew accustomed to the peculiarities of the district, they went even slower than their quarry, with the result that they steadily overhauled them. It was like a race in reverse—a go-slow race.

On and on the strange procession went, farther and farther into the dazzling white glow, weaving back and forth through the dream streets until it came to the corner of Never Lane.

Cassiopeia turned into the lane and crawled toward Nowhere House. Momo, remembering that she'd failed to make any headway until she turned around and walked backward, did the same again.

And that was when her heart stood still.

The time-thieves, like a gray wall on the move, stretched away for as far as the eye could see, rank upon rank of them filling the entire width of the street.

Momo cried out in terror, but she couldn't hear her own voice. She walked backward down Never Lane, staring wide-eyed at the advancing host of men in gray.

But then another strange thing happened. As soon as the leaders tried to enter the lane, they vanished before her very eyes. Their outstretched hands were the first to disappear, then their legs and bodies, and last of all their faces, which wore a look of surprise and horror.

But Momo wasn't the only one to have witnessed this phenomenon. It had also been seen by the men in gray who were following behind. They shrank back, bracing themselves to resist the pressure of those still advancing in the rear, and something of a scuffle ensued. Momo saw her pursuers scowl and shake their fists, but they dared not pursue her any farther.

At last she reached Nowhere House. The big bronze door swung open. She darted inside, raced down the corridor lined with statues, opened the tiny door at the other end, ducked through it, ran across the great hall to the little room enclosed by grandfather clocks, threw herself down on the dainty little sofa, and, not wanting to see or hear anything more, buried her head under a cushion.

NINETEEN

Under Siege

A GENTLE VOICE was speaking.

Momo emerged by degrees from the depths of a dreamless sleep, feeling wonderfully rested and refreshed. "Momo isn't to blame," she heard the voice say, "but you, Cassiopeia—you should have known better."

Momo opened her eyes. Professor Hora was sitting at the little table in front of the sofa, looking ruefully down at the tortoise. "Didn't it occur to you," he went on, "that the men in gray might follow you?"

There wasn't room on Cassiopeia's shell for all she had to say, so she had to reply in three installments: I CAN ONLY SEE —HALF AN HOUR AHEAD—TOO LATE BY THEN.

Professor Hora sighed and shook his head. "Oh, Cassiopeia, Cassiopeia, even I find you puzzling sometimes."

Momo sat up.

"Ah, our guest is awake," Professor Hora said kindly. "I hope you're feeling better?"

"Much better, thank you," said Momo. "Please excuse me for falling asleep on your sofa."

The professor smiled. "It's quite all right, you've no need to apologize. Cassiopeia has already brought me up to date on anything I failed to see through my omnivision glasses."

"What are the men in gray doing?" Momo asked anxiously.

Professor Hora produced a big blue handkerchief from his pocket. "We're under siege. They have us completely surrounded—that's to say, they're as close to Nowhere House as they can get."

"But they can't get in, can they?" Momo said.

The professor blew his nose. "No, they can't. You saw for yourself, they vanish into thin air if they so much as set foot in Never Lane."

Momo looked mystified. "Yes, but I don't know why."

"It's temporal suction that does it," the professor told her. "Everything has to be done backward in Never Lane, as you know, because time runs in reverse around this house. Normally, time flows into you. The more time you have inside you, the older you get, but in Never Lane time flows out of you. You grew younger while you were coming up the lane. Not much younger—only as much younger as the time you took to get from one end to the other."

"I didn't notice anything," Momo said, still mystified.

"That's because you're a human being," the professor said with a smile. "There's a lot more to human beings than the time they carry around inside them, but it's different with the men in gray. Stolen time is all they consist of, and that disappears in a flash when they're exposed to temporal suction. It escapes like air from a burst balloon, the only difference being that a balloon's skin survives. In their case, there's nothing left at all."

Momo knit her brow and thought hard. "Wouldn't it be possible," she asked at length, "to make time run backward all over the world? Only for a little while, I mean. It wouldn't matter if people grew a tiny bit younger, but the time-thieves would be reduced to nothing."

The professor smiled again. "A splendid idea, I grant you, but I'm afraid it wouldn't work. The two currents are in balance, you see. If you canceled one, the other would vanish too. Then there'd be no time left . . ."

He broke off and pushed his omnivision glasses up so that they rested on his forehead.

"On the other hand . . ." he murmured. Momo watched him expectantly as he paced up and down the room a few times, lost in thought, and Cassiopeia followed him with her wise old eyes. At length he sat down again.

"You've given me an idea," he said, "but I couldn't put it into practice unaided." He looked down at the tortoise. "Cassiopeia, my dear, I'd like your opinion on something. What's the best thing to do when you're under siege?"

HAVE BREAKFAST, came the reply.

"Quite so," said the professor. "That's another splendid idea."

The table was laid in a flash. Whether or not it had been laid all the time and Momo simply hadn't noticed, everything was in place: the two little cups, the pot of steaming chocolate, the honey, butter, and crusty rolls.

Momo, whose mouth had often watered at the recollection of her first delicious, golden-hued breakfast at Nowhere House, dug in at once. Everything tasted even better than before, if possible, and this time the professor dug in heartily too.

"Professor," Momo said after a while, with her cheeks still bulging, "they want you to give them all the time that exists. You won't, though, will you?"

"No, child," he replied, "that I'll never do. Time will come to an end someday, but not until people don't need it any longer. The men in gray won't get any time from me—not even a split second."

"But they say they can *make* you hand it over," Momo said.

"Before we go into that," the professor told her, very gravely, "I'd like you to look at them for yourself."

All she saw to begin with was the kaleidoscope of colors and shapes that had made her so dizzy the first time, but it wasn't

long before her eyes got used to the omnivision lenses. And then the besieging army swam into focus!

The men in gray were drawn up in a long, long line, shoulder to shoulder, not only across the mouth of Never Lane but all around the district with the snow-white houses. They formed an unbroken cordon, and the midpoint of that cordon was Nowhere House.

But then Momo noticed something else—something strange. Her first thought was that the lenses of the omnivision glasses needed polishing, or that she hadn't quite grown used to them yet, because the outlines of the men in gray looked misty. She soon realized that this blurring had nothing to do with the lenses or her eyes: the mist was real, and it was rising from the streets all around, dense and impenetrable in some places, only just forming in others.

The men in gray were standing absolutely still, all wearing derbies and carrying briefcases, and all smoking little gray cigars. But the smoke from the cigars didn't disperse in the normal way. Here, where the air seemed made of glass and was never disturbed by a breath of wind, the threads of smoke clung like cobwebs, creeping along the streets and up the walls of the snow-white houses, festooning each ledge and cornice and windowsill, condensing into a noisome, bluish green fogbank that billowed ever higher until it encircled Nowhere House like a wall.

Momo took off the glasses and looked at Professor Hora inquiringly.

"Have you seen enough?" he asked. "Then let me have the glasses back." He put them on again. "You asked if the men in gray could make me do something against my will," he went on. "Well, they can't get at me personally, as you know, but they could subject the world to an evil far worse than any they've inflicted on it so far. That's how they hope to force my hand."

Momo was appalled. "What could be worse than stealing people's time?" she asked.

"I allot people their share of time," the professor explained. "The men in gray can't stop that. They can't intercept the time I distribute, but they can poison it."

"They can *poison* it?" Momo repeated, more appalled still.

The professor nodded. "Yes, with the smoke from their cigars. Have you ever seen one without his little gray cigar? Of course not, because without it he couldn't exist."

"What kind of cigars are they?" Momo asked.

"You remember where the hour-lilies were growing?" Professor Hora said. "I told you then that everyone has a place like that, because everyone has a heart. If people allow the men in gray to gain a foothold there, more and more of their hour-lilies get stolen. But hour-lilies plucked from a person's heart can't die, because they've never really withered. They can't live, either, because they've been parted from their rightful owner. They strive with every fiber of their being to return to the person they belong to."

Momo was listening with bated breath.

"If you think I know everything, Momo, you're wrong. Some evils are wrapped in mystery. I've no idea where the men in gray keep their stolen hour-lilies. I only know that they preserve the blossoms by freezing them till they're as hard as glass goblets. Somewhere far below ground there must be a gigantic cold store."

Momo's cheeks began to burn with indignation.

"And that's where the men in gray draw their supplies from. They pull off the hour-lilies' petals, let them wither till they're dried up and gray, and roll their little cigars out of them. The petals still contain remnants of life, even then, but living time is harmful to the men in gray, so they light the cigars and smoke them. Only when time has been converted into smoke is it well and truly dead. That's what keeps the men in gray 'alive': dead human time."

Momo had risen to her feet. "Oh," she exclaimed, "to think of all those poor flowers, all that dead time . . ."

"Yes, the wall they're erecting around this house is built of dead time. There's still enough open sky above for me to send people their time in good condition, but once that pall of smoke closes over our heads, every hour I send them will be contaminated with the time-thieves' poison. When they absorb it, it'll make them ill."

Momo stared at the professor uncomprehendingly. "What kind of illness is it?" she asked in a low voice.

"A fatal illness, though you scarcely notice it at first. One day, you don't feel like doing anything. Nothing interests you, everything bores you. Far from wearing off, your boredom persists and gets worse, day by day and week by week. You feel more and more bad-tempered, more and more empty inside, more and more dissatisfied with yourself and the world in general. Then even that feeling wears off, and you don't feel anything anymore. You become completely indifferent to what goes on around you. Joy and sorrow, anger and excitement are things of the past. You forget how to laugh and cry—you're cold inside and incapable of loving anything or anyone. Once you reach that stage, the disease is incurable. There's no going back. You bustle around with a blank, gray face, just like the men in gray themselves—indeed, you've joined their ranks. The disease has a name. It's called deadly tedium."

Momo shivered. "You mean," she said, "unless you hand over all the time there is, they'll turn people into creatures like themselves?"

"Yes," the professor replied. "That's how they hope to bully me into it." He rose and turned away. "I've waited till now for people to get rid of those pests. They could have done so—after all, it was they who brought them into existence in the first place—but I can't wait any longer. I must do something, and I can't do it on my own." He looked Momo in the eye. "Will you help me?"

"Yes," she whispered.

"If you do, you'll be running an incalculable risk. It will be up to you whether the world begins to live again or stands still forever and a day. Are you really prepared to take that risk?"

"Yes," Momo repeated, and this time her voice was firm.

"In that case," said the professor, "listen carefully to what I'm going to tell you, because you'll be all on your own. I won't be able to help you, nor will anyone else."

Momo nodded, gazing at him intently.

"I must begin by telling you that I never sleep," he said. "If I dozed off, time would stand still and the world would come to a stop. If there were no more time, the men in gray would have none left to steal. They could continue to exist for a while by using up their vast reserves, but once those had gone they would dissolve into thin air."

"Then the answer's simple, surely?" said Momo.

"Not as simple as it sounds, I'm afraid, or I wouldn't need your help. The trouble is, if there were no more time I couldn't wake up again, and the world would continue to stand still for all eternity. It does, however, lie within my power to give you—and you alone—an hour-lily. Only one, of course, because only one ever blooms at a time. So, if time stopped all over the world, you would still have one hour's grace."

"Then I could wake you," said Momo.

The professor shook his head. "That would achieve nothing, because the men in gray have far too much time in reserve. They would consume very little of it in an hour, so they'd still be there when the hour was up. No, Momo, the problem is a great deal harder than that. As soon as the men in gray notice that time has stopped—and it won't take them long, because their supply of cigars will be interrupted— they'll lift the siege and head for their secret store. You must follow them and prevent them from reaching it. When their cigars are finished, they'll be finished too. But then comes what may well turn out to be the hardest part of all. Once the last of the time-thieves has vanished, you must release every stolen minute, because only when people get their time back will I wake up and the world come to life again. And all this you'll have to do within the space of a single hour."

Momo hadn't reckoned with such a host of difficulties and dangers. She stared at him helplessly.

"Will you try all the same?" the professor asked. "It's our only chance."

Momo couldn't bring herself to speak, she found the prospect so daunting. At that moment, Cassiopeia's shell lit up. I'LL COME TOO, it signaled.

Unlikely as it seemed that the tortoise could be of help, the words conjured up a tiny ray of hope. Momo felt heartened at the thought of not being entirely alone. Although there were no rational grounds for such a feeling, it did at least enable her to make up her mind.

"I'll try," she said resolutely.

Professor Hora gave her a long look and started to smile. "Many things will prove easier than you think. You've heard the music of the stars. You mustn't feel frightened." He turned to the tortoise. "So you want to go too, do you?"

OF COURSE, Cassiopeia spelled out. Then, SOMEONE HAS TO LOOK AFTER HER.

The professor and Momo smiled at each other.

"Will she get an hour-lily too?" Momo asked.

"She doesn't need one," the professor replied, gently tickling the tortoise's neck. "Cassiopeia is a creature from beyond the frontiers of time. She carries her own little supply of time inside her. She could go on crawling across the face of the earth even if everything else stood still forever."

"Good," said Momo, suddenly eager to get on with the job. "What happens next?"

"Now," said the professor, "we say goodbye."

Momo felt a lump in her throat. "Won't we ever see each other again?" she asked softly.

"Of course we will," he told her, "and until that day comes, every hour of your life will bring you my love. We'll always be friends, won't we?"

Momo nodded.

"I'm going now," the professor went on, "but you mustn't follow me or ask where I'm going. My sleep is no ordinary sleep, and I'd sooner you weren't there. One last thing: as soon as I'm gone, you must open both doors, the little one with my name on it and the big bronze one that leads into Never Lane. Once time has stopped, everything will stand still and no power on earth will be able to budge those doors. Have you understood and memorized all I've told you?"

"Yes," said Momo, "but how shall I know when time has stopped?"

"You'll know, never fear."

They both stood up. Professor Hora gently stroked Momo's tousled mop of hair. "Goodbye, Momo," he said, "and thank you for listening so carefully."

"I'm going to tell everyone about you," she replied, "when it's all over."

From one moment to the next, Professor Hora looked as old as he had when he carried her into the golden dome—as old as an ancient tree or primeval crag.

Turning away, he walked swiftly out of the little room whose walls consisted of grandfather clocks. Momo heard his footsteps fade until they were indistinguishable from the ticking of the countless clocks around her. Their incessant whirring and ticking and chiming seemed to have swallowed him up.

Momo took Cassiopeia in her arms and held her tight. Her great adventure had begun. There could be no turning back.

TWENTY

Pursuing the Pursuers

MOMO'S FIRST STEP was to open the little door with Professor Hora's name on it. Then she sped along the corridor lined with statues and opened the big bronze front door. She had to exert all her strength because it was so heavy.

That done, she ran back to the great hall and waited, with Cassiopeia in her arms, to see what would happen.

She didn't have to wait long. There was a sudden jolt, but it didn't actually shake the ground. It was a timequake, so to speak, not an earthquake. No words could describe the sensation, which was accompanied by a sound such as no human ear had ever heard before: a sigh that seemed to issue from the depths of the ages.

And then it was over.

Simultaneously, the innumerable clocks stopped ticking, whirring, and chiming. Pendulums came to a sudden halt and stayed put at odd angles. The silence that fell was more profound than any that had ever reigned before. Time itself was standing still.

As for Momo, she became aware that she was clasping the

stem of an hour-lily of exceptional size and beauty. She hadn't felt anyone put it into her hand. It simply appeared, as if it had always been there.

Gingerly, Momo took a step. Sure enough, she could move as easily as ever. The remains of breakfast were still on the table. She sat down on one of the little armchairs, but the seat was as hard as marble and didn't yield an inch. There was a mouthful of chocolate left in her cup, but the cup wouldn't move either. She tried dipping her fingers in the dregs, but they were as hard as butterscotch. So was the honey, and even the crumbs were stuck fast to the plates. Now that time had stopped, everything else was immovable too.

Cassiopeia had started to fidget. Looking down, Momo saw some words on her shell. YOU'RE WASTING TIME! she read.

Heavens alive, so she was! Momo pulled herself together. She hurried through the forest of clocks to the little door, squeezed through it, and ran along the passage to the front door. She peered out, then darted back in panic. Her heart began to thump furiously. Far from running away, the time-thieves were streaming toward her up Never Lane. They could do that, of course, now time had ceased to flow in reverse there, but she hadn't allowed for the possibility.

She raced back to the great hall and, still clutching Cassiopeia, hid behind a massive grandfather clock. "That's a good start," she muttered ruefully.

Then she heard the men in gray come marching along the corridor. They squeezed through the little door, one after another, until a whole crowd of them had assembled inside.

"So this is our new headquarters," said one, surveying the vast room. "Very impressive."

"That girl let us in," said another gray voice. "I distinctly saw her open the door, the sensible child. I wonder how she managed to get around the old man."

"If you ask me," said a third voice, "the old man's knuckled under. If time has stopped flowing in Never Lane, it can only mean he switched it off himself. In other words, he knows he's beaten. Where is he, the old mischief-maker? Let's finish him off!"

The men in gray were looking around when one of them had a sudden thought. His voice sounded even grayer, if possible, than the rest. "Something's wrong, gentlemen," he said. "The clocks—look at the clocks! Every one of them has stopped, even this hourglass here."

"I suppose he must have stopped them," another voice said uncertainly.

"You can't stop an hourglass," the first man in gray retorted. "See for yourselves, gentlemen—the sand's suspended in midair and the hourglass itself won't budge! What does it mean?"

He was still speaking when footsteps came pounding along the corridor and yet another man in gray squeezed through the little door, gesticulating wildly. "We've just had word from our agents in the city," he announced. "Their cars have stopped, and so has everything else—the world's at a standstill. There isn't a microsecond of time to be had anywhere. Our supplies have been cut off. Time has ceased to exist. Hora has switched it off!"

There was a deathly hush. Then someone said, "What do you mean, switched it off? What'll become of us when we've finished the cigars we're smoking?"

"What'll become of us?" shouted someone else. "You know that perfectly well. This is disastrous, gentlemen!"

They all began to shout at once. "Hora's planning to destroy us!"—"We must lift the siege at once!"—"We must try to reach the time store!"—"Without our cars? We'll never make it in time!"—"My cigar won't last me more than twenty-seven minutes!"—"Mine will last me forty-eight!"—"Give it to me, then!"—"Are you crazy? It's every man for himself!"

There was a concerted rush for the little door. From her hiding place, Momo saw panic-stricken gray figures trying to squeeze through it, jostling, scuffling, and swapping punches in a desperate attempt to save their gray lives. The rush became a violent melee as they knocked each other's hats off, wrestled with each other, snatched the cigars from each other's mouths. And whenever they lost their cigars, they seemed to lose every ounce of strength as well. They stood there with their arms outstretched and a plaintive, terrified expression on their faces, growing more and more transparent until they finally vanished. Nothing remained of them, not even their hats.

In the end, only three men in gray were left. They ducked through the little door, one after the other, and scuttled off down the passage.

Momo, with Cassiopeia under one arm and her free hand tightly clutching the hour-lily, ran after them. All now depended on her keeping them in sight.

She saw, when she emerged from the front door, that they had already reached the mouth of Never Lane. More smoke-wreathed men in gray were standing there, talking and gesticulating excitedly. As soon as they caught sight of the three fugitives from Nowhere House, they started running too. Others joined in the stampede, and soon the whole army had taken to its heels. "More haste less speed" no longer applied, of course, now that time was at a standstill. An endless column of gray figures streamed toward the city through the strange, dreamlike district with its snow-white houses and oddly assorted shadows, past the monument resembling an egg, until it came to the gray, shabby tenements inhabited by people who lived on the edge of time. Here too, though, everything was still and silent.

What followed was a chase in reverse—a chase in which countless gray figures were pursued through the city, at a discreet distance behind the last of the stragglers, by a girl with a flower in her hand and a tortoise under her arm.

But how strange the city looked now! Long lines of cars choked the streets with the fumes from their exhausts solidified, and behind each wheel sat a motionless driver, one hand frozen on horn or gear shift. Momo even caught sight of one driver who had been immobilized while glaring at his neighbor and meaningfully tapping his forehead. Cyclists were poised at road junctions with their arms extended, signaling right or left, and the people thronging the sidewalks resembled waxwork figures.

Traffic cops stood at intersections, whistles in their mouths, caught in the act of waving the traffic on. A flock of pigeons hovered motionless above a square, and high overhead, as though painted on the sky, was an equally motionless airplane. The water in the fountains might have been ice, leaves falling from trees were suspended in midair, and one little dog, which was cocking its leg against a lamppost, looked as if it had been stuffed that way.

Lifeless as a photograph, the city rang to the hurrying footsteps of the men in gray. Momo followed them cautiously, fearful of being spotted, but she needn't have worried. Their headlong flight was proving so arduous and exhausting that they had ceased to notice anything anymore.

Unaccustomed to running so far and so fast, they panted and gasped for breath, grimly clenching their teeth on the little gray cigars that kept them in existence. More than one of them let his cigar fall while running and vanished into thin air before he could retrieve it.

But their companions in misfortune represented an even greater threat. Such was the desperation of those whose own cigars were almost finished that many of them snatched the butts from their neighbors' mouths, so their numbers slowly but steadily dwindled.

Those who still had a small store of cigars in their briefcases were careful to conceal them from the others, because the have-nots kept hurling themselves at the haves and trying to wrest their precious possessions from them. Scores of struggling figures engaged in ferocious tussles, scrabbling and clawing with such wild abandon that most of the coveted cigars spilled onto the roadway and were trampled underfoot. The men in gray had become so frightened of extinction that they completely lost their heads.

There was something else that caused them increasing difficulty the farther into town they got. The streets were so crowded at many points that it was all they could do to thread their way through the forest of motionless pedestrians. Momo, being small and thin, had an easier time of it, but even she had to watch her step. You could hurt yourself badly on a feather suspended in midair if you ran into it by mistake.

On and on they went, and Momo still had no idea how much farther it was to the time store. She peered anxiously at her hour-lily, but it had only just come into full flower. There was no need to worry yet.

Then something happened that temporarily drove every other thought from her mind. Glancing down a side street, she caught sight of Beppo!

"Beppo!" she called, beside herself with joy, as she ran toward him. "I've been looking for you everywhere. Where have you been all this time? Oh, Beppo, dearest Beppo!"

Still clutching Cassiopeia, she flung her free arm around his neck—and promptly bounced off, because he might have been made of cast iron. It was such a painful collision that tears sprang to her eyes. She stepped back, sobbing, and gazed at him.

The little old man looked more bent-backed than ever. His kindly face was thin and gaunt and very pale, and his chin was frosted with white stubble because he so seldom found the time to shave nowadays. Incessant sweeping had worn away his broom until the bristles were little longer than his beard. There he stood, as motionless as everyone and everything else, staring down at the dirty street through his steel-rimmed spectacles.

Momo had found him at last, but only now, when she couldn't get him to notice her and it might be the very last time she saw him. If things went wrong, old Beppo would continue to stand there forevermore.

Cassiopeia started fidgeting again. KEEP GOING! she spelled.

Momo dashed back to the main street and stopped dead. There were no men in gray to be seen! She ran on a little way, but it was no use, she'd lost track of them. She halted again, wondering what to do, and looked inquiringly at Cassiopeia.

KEEP GOING, the tortoise signaled: YOU'LL FIND THEM.

If Cassiopeia knew in advance that she would find the time-thieves, she would find them whichever way she went. Any direction was bound to be the right one, so she simply ran on, turning left or right as the fancy took her.

She had now reached the housing development on the city's northern outskirts, where the buildings were as alike as peas in a pod and the streets ran dead straight from horizon to horizon. On and on she ran, but the sheer sameness of the buildings and streets soon made her feel as if she were running on the spot and getting nowhere. The housing development was a veritable maze, but a maze that deceived one by its regularity and uniformity.

Momo had almost lost hope when she caught sight of a man in gray disappearing around a corner. He was limping along with his suit in tatters and his derby and briefcase gone, mouth grimly pursed around the smoldering butt of a cigar.

She followed him along a street flanked by endless rows of houses until they came to a gap. The big rectangular site where the missing house should have stood was boarded up, and set in the fence was a gate. The gate was a little ajar, and the last gray straggler squeezed quickly through it.

There was a notice above the gate. Momo paused to read it.

TWENTY-ONE

An End and a Beginning

MOMO TOOK SEVERAL SECONDS to decipher the longer words on the notice board, and by the time she slipped through the gate the last of the men in gray had disappeared.

In front of her yawned a gigantic pit, eighty or ninety feet deep, with bulldozers and excavators around it. Several trucks had stopped midway down the ramp that led to the bottom of the pit, and construction workers were standing motionless all over the place, frozen in a variety of positions.

Where to now? There was no sign of the man in gray and no clue to where he might have gone. Cassiopeia seemed equally at a loss. Her shell did not light up.

Momo made her way down the ramp to the bottom of the pit and looked around. Suddenly she saw a familiar face. It was Salvatore, the bricklayer who had painted the pretty flower picture on the wall of her room. He was as motionless as all the rest, but something about his pose made Momo think twice. He was cupping his mouth as though calling to someone and pointing to the rim of a huge pipe jutting from the ground beside him, almost as if drawing Momo's attention to it.

Momo wasted no time. Taking this as a good omen, she hurried over to the pipe and climbed inside. She lost her footing almost at once, because the pipe sloped downward at a steep angle, twisting and turning so sharply that she slithered back and forth like a child on a helter-skelter. She could see and hear almost nothing as she hurtled ever deeper into the ground, sometimes sliding on her bottom, sometimes rolling head over heels, but never letting go of the tortoise and the hour-lily.

The deeper she went, the colder it became. She began to wonder how she would ever get out again, but before she could give the problem any real thought the pipe abruptly ended in an underground passage. It wasn't as dark here. The tunnel was bathed in a gray twilight that seemed to ooze from its very walls.

Momo scrambled up and ran on. Her bare feet made no sound, but she could hear footsteps ahead of her. Guessing that they belonged to the men in gray, she allowed herself to be guided by them. To judge by the innumerable passages leading off her own in all directions, she was in a maze of tunnels that ran the full extent of the housing development.

Then she heard a babble of voices. Having traced the hubbub to its source, she cautiously peeped around the corner.

She found herself looking at a room as vast as the conference table that ran down the middle of it, and at this table, in two long rows, sat the surviving men in gray. Momo almost felt sorry for them, they looked so woebegone. Their suits were torn, their bald gray heads cut and bruised, and their faces convulsed with fear, but their cigars were still smoldering.

Embedded in the wall at the far end of the room, Momo saw a huge steel door. The door was ajar, and an icy draft was streaming from whatever lay beyond. Although Momo knew it would do little good, she hunkered down and tucked her bare feet under her skirt.

A man in gray was presiding at the head of the conference table, just in front of the strong-room door. "We must economize," Momo heard him say. "Our reserves must be carefully husbanded. After all, we don't know how long they'll have to last us."

"There's only a handful of us left," cried someone. "They'll last us for years."

"The sooner we start economizing," the chairman went on imperturbably, "the longer we'll hold out. I don't have to tell you, gentlemen, what I mean by economizing. It will be quite sufficient if only *some* of us survive this disaster. Let's face facts. As things stand now, there are far too many of us. Common sense dictates that our ranks be drastically thinned. May I ask you to number off?"

When the men in gray had numbered off, all around the table, the chairman produced a coin from his pocket. "I shall now toss up," he said. "Heads means the even numbers survive, tails the odd numbers."

He flipped the coin and caught it.

"Heads," he announced. "Even numbers may remain seated, odd numbers are requested to dissolve forthwith."

The losers emitted a dull groan, but none of them demurred. As soon as the winners had relieved them of their cigars, they vanished into thin air.

The chairman's voice broke the hush. "And now, gentlemen, kindly do the same again."

The same gruesome procedure was followed a second time, then a third and a fourth, until only half a dozen men in gray remained. They sat at the head of the conference table, three on each side, and glared across it in icy silence.

Momo, who had watched these developments with horrified fascination, noticed that the temperature rose appreciably every time another batch of losers disappeared. Compared to what it had been before, the cold was quite tolerable.

"Six," remarked one of the survivors, "is an unlucky number."

"That's enough," said another. "There's no point in reducing our numbers still further. If six of us can't survive this disaster, neither will three."

"Not necessarily," said someone else, "but we can always review the situation if need arises—later, I mean."

No one spoke for a while. Then another survivor said, "Lucky for us the door to the time store was open when disaster struck. If it had been shut at the crucial moment, no power on earth could open it now. We'd be absolutely sunk."

"You're not entirely right, I'm afraid," replied another. "Because the door is open, cold is escaping from the refrigeration plant. The hour-lilies will slowly thaw out, and you all know what'll happen then. We won't be able to prevent them from returning to their original owners."

"You mean," said yet another, "that our own coldness won't be sufficient to keep them deep-frozen?"

"There are only six of us, unfortunately," said the second speaker. "You can calculate our freezing capability for yourself. Personally, I feel it was rather rash to cut down our numbers so drastically. It hasn't paid off."

"We had to opt for one course of action or the other," snapped the first speaker, "and we did, so that's that."

Another silence fell.

"In other words," said someone, "we may have to sit here for years on end, twiddling our thumbs and gaping at each other. I find that a dismal prospect, I must confess."

Momo racked her brains. There was certainly no point in her sitting there and waiting any longer. When the men in gray were gone, the hour-lilies would thaw out by themselves, but the men in gray still existed and would continue to exist unless she did something about it. But what *could* she do, given that the door to the cold store was open and the time-thieves could help themselves to fresh supplies of cigars whenever they wanted?

At that moment, Cassiopeia nudged her in the ribs. Momo looked down and saw a message on her shell. SHUT THE DOOR, she read.

"I can't," she whispered back. "I'd never move it."

USE THE FLOWER, Cassiopeia replied.

"You mean I could move it if I touched it with the hour-lily?" whispered Momo.

YES, AND YOU WILL, the tortoise spelled out.

If Cassiopeia knew this in advance, it had to be true. Momo carefully put the tortoise down. Then she took the hour-lily, which was wilting by now and had lost most of its petals, and stowed it inside her jacket.

Going down on all fours, she sneaked unseen beneath the conference table and crawled to the far end. By the time she was on a level with the time-thieves' six pairs of legs, her heart was pounding fit to burst.

Very, very gingerly, she took out the hour-lily and, gripping the stem between her teeth, crawled on. Still unobserved by the men in gray, she reached the open door, touched it with the hour-lily, and simultaneously gave it a push. The well-oiled hinges didn't make a sound. The door swung silently to, then shut with a mighty clang that went echoing around the conference chamber and reverberated from the walls of the innumerable underground passages.

Momo jumped to her feet. The men in gray, who hadn't the remotest idea that anyone but themselves was exempt from the universal standstill, sat rooted to their chairs in horror, staring at her.

Without a second thought, she dashed past them and sprinted back to the exit. The men in gray recovered from their shock and raced after her.

"It's that frightful little girl!" she heard one of them shout. "It's Momo!"

"Impossible!" yelled another. "The creature's moving!"

"She's got an hour-lily!" bellowed a third.

"Is that how she moved the door?" asked a fourth.

The fifth smote his brow. "Then we could have moved it ourselves. We've got plenty of hour-lilies."

"We did have, you mean!" screamed the sixth. "Only one thing can save us now that the door's shut. If we don't get hold of that flower of hers, we're done for!"

Meanwhile, Momo had already disappeared into the maze of tunnels. The men in gray knew their way around better, of course, but she just managed to elude them by zigzagging to and fro.

Cassiopeia played her own special part in this chase. Although she could only crawl, she always knew in advance where Momo's pursuers would go next, so she got there in good time and stationed herself in their path. The men in gray tripped over her and went sprawling, and the ones behind tripped over them and went sprawling too, with the result that she more than once saved Momo from almost certain capture. Although she herself was often sent hurtling against walls by flying feet, nothing could deter her from continuing to do what she knew in advance she would do.

As the chase proceeded, several of the pursuing men in gray became so maddened by their craving for the hour-lily that they dropped their cigars and vanished into thin air, one after the other. In the end, only two were left.

Momo doubled back and took refuge in the conference chamber. The two surviving time-thieves chased her around the table but failed to catch her, so they split up and ran in opposite directions. Momo was trapped at last. She cowered in a corner and gazed at her pursuers in terror with the hour-lily clasped to her chest. All but three of its shimmering petals had withered and fallen.

The foremost man in gray was just about to snatch the flower when the other one yanked him away.

"No," he shrieked, "that flower's mine! Mine, I tell you!"

They grappled with each other, and in the ensuing scrimmage the first man knocked the second man's cigar out of his mouth. With a weird groan, the second man spun around, went transparent, and vanished.

The last of the men in gray advanced on Momo with a minuscule cigar butt smoldering in the corner of his mouth.

"Give it here!" he gasped, but as he did so the butt fell out of his mouth and rolled away under the table. He flung himself to the ground and groped for it, but it eluded his outstretched fingers. Turning his ashen face toward Momo, he struggled into a sitting position and raised one trembling hand.

"Please," he whispered faintly, "please, dear child, give me the flower."

Momo, still cowering in her corner, couldn't get a word out. She clasped the flower still tighter and shook her head.

The last of the men in gray nodded slowly. "I'm glad," he murmured. "I'm glad . . . it's all . . . over . . ."

Then he vanished too.

Momo was staring dazedly at the place where he had been when Cassiopeia crawled into view. YOU'LL OPEN THE DOOR, her shell announced.

Momo went over to the door, touched it with her hour-lily, which had only one last petal left, and opened it wide.

The time store was cold no longer, now that the last of the time-thieves had gone. Momo marveled at the contents of the huge vault. Innumerable hour-lilies were arrayed on its endless shelves like crystal goblets, no two alike and each more beautiful than the other. Hundreds of thousands, indeed, millions of hours were stored here, all of them stolen from people's lives.

The temperature steadily rose until the vault was as hot as a greenhouse. Just as the last petal of Momo's hour-lily fluttered to the ground, all the other flowers left their shelves in clouds and swirled around her head. It was like a warm spring storm, but a storm made up of time released from captivity.

As if in a dream, Momo looked around and saw Cassiopeia on the ground beside her. The glowing letters on her shell read: FLY HOME, MOMO, FLY HOME!

That was the last Momo ever saw of Cassiopeia, because the tempest of flowers rose to an indescribable pitch. And as it gained strength, so Momo was lifted off her feet and borne away like a flower herself, along the dark passages, out into the open air, and high above the city. Soaring over the roofs in a cloud of flowers that grew bigger every moment, she was wafted up and down and around and around like someone performing a triumphal dance to glorious music.

Then the cloud of flowers drifted slowly, lazily down and landed like snowflakes on the frozen face of the earth. And, like snowflakes, they gently dissolved and became invisible as they returned to their true home in the hearts of mankind.

In that same moment, time began again and everything awoke to new life. The cars drove on, the traffic cops blew their whistles, the pigeons continued circling, and the little dog made a puddle against the lamppost. Nobody noticed that time had stood still for an hour, because nothing had moved in the interval. It was all over in the twinkling of an eye.

Nothing had moved—no, but something had changed. All of a sudden, people found they had plenty of time to spare. They were delighted, naturally, but they never realized that it was their own time that had miraculously been restored to them.

When Momo came to her senses again, she found herself back in the side street where she had last seen Beppo. Sure enough, there he was, leaning on his broom with his back to her, gazing ruminatively into the distance as he used to in the old days. He wasn't in a hurry anymore, and for some unknown reason he felt brighter and more hopeful.

"I wonder," he thought. "Maybe I've already saved the hundred thousand hours I need to ransom Momo."

At that moment, someone tugged at his jacket and he turned to see Momo smiling up at him as large as life.

There are no words to describe the joy of that reunion. Beppo and Momo laughed and cried by turns, and they both kept talking at once—talking all kinds of nonsense, too, as people do when they're dazed with delight. They hugged each other again and again, and passersby paused to share in their happiness, their tears and laughter, because they all had plenty of time to spare.

At long last, Beppo shouldered his broom—he took the rest of the day off, of course—and the two of them strolled arm in arm through the city to the old amphitheater, still talking a mile a minute.

It was a long time since the city had witnessed such scenes. Children played in the middle of the street, getting in the way of cars whose drivers not only watched and waited, smiling broadly, but sometimes got out and joined in their games. People stood around chatting with the friendliness of those who take a genuine interest in their neighbors' welfare. Other people, on their way to work, had time to stop and admire the flowers in a window box or feed the birds. Doctors, too, had time to devote themselves properly to their patients, and workers of all kinds did their jobs with pride and loving care, now that they were no longer expected to turn out as much work as possible in the shortest possible time. They could take as much time as they needed and wanted, because from now on there was enough time for everyone.

Many people never discovered whom they had to thank for all this, just as they never knew what had actually happened during the hour that passed in a flash. Few of them would have believed the story anyway.

The only ones that knew and believed it were Momo's friends. By the time Momo and Beppo reached the amphitheater, they were all there waiting: Guido, Paolo, Massimo, Franco, Maria and her little sister Rosa, Claudio and a host of other children, Nino the innkeeper and his plump wife Liliana and their baby, Salvatore the bricklayer, and all of Momo's regular visitors in days gone by.

The celebration that followed, which was as merry and joyous as only Momo's friends could have made it, went on till the stars came out. And when all the cheers and hugs and handshakes and excited chatter had subsided, everyone sat down on the grass-grown steps.

A great hush fell as Momo stepped out into the middle of the arena. She thought of the music of the stars and the hour-lilies, and then, in a sweet, pure voice, she began to sing.

Meanwhile, in Nowhere House, the return of time had roused Professor Hora from his first sleep ever. Still very pale, he looked as if he had just recovered from a serious illness, but his eyes sparkled and there was a smile on his lips as he watched Momo and her friends through his omnivision glasses.

Then he felt something touch his foot. Taking off his glasses, he looked down and saw Cassiopeia sitting there.

"Cassiopeia," he said, tickling her affectionately under the chin, "the two of you did a fine job. I couldn't watch you, for once, so you must tell me all about it."

LATER, the tortoise signaled. Then she sneezed.

The professor looked concerned. "You haven't caught cold, have you?"

YOU BET I HAVE! replied Cassiopeia.

"You must have gone too close to the men in gray," said the professor. "I expect you're very tired, too. We can talk later. Better go off and have a good sleep first."

THANKS, came the answer.

Cassiopeia limped off and picked herself a nice, dark, quiet corner. She tucked her head and legs in, and very slowly, in letters visible only to those who have read this story, her shell spelled out two words:

Author's Postscript

Many of my readers may have questions they'd like to ask. If so, I'm afraid I can't help them. The fact is, I wrote this story down from memory, just as it was told me. I never met Momo or any of her friends, nor do I know what became of them or how they are today. As for the city where they lived, I can only guess which one it was.

The most I can tell you is this:

One night in a train, while I was on a long journey (as I still am), I found myself sitting opposite a remarkable fellow passenger—remarkable in that I found it quite impossible to tell his age. At first I put him down as an old man, but I soon saw that I must have been mistaken, because he suddenly seemed very young—though that impression, too, soon proved to be false.

At any rate, it was he who told me the story during our long night's journey together.

Neither of us spoke for some moments after he had finished. Then my mysterious acquaintance made a remark which I feel bound to put on record. "I've described all these events," he said, "as if they'd already happened. I might just as well have described them as if they still lay in the future. To me, there's very little difference."

He must have left the train at the next station, because I noticed after a while that I was alone.

I've never bumped into him again, unfortunately. If by any chance I do, though, I shall have plenty of questions to ask him myself.